William Shakespeare's
King Lear
In Plain and Simple English

BOOKCAPS

BookCaps Study Guides
www.bookcaps.com

© 2011. All Rights Reserved.

Table of Contents:

- **CHARACTERS** 4
- **ACT 1** 5
  - SCENE I. King Lear's palace. 6
  - SCENE II. The Earl of Gloucester's castle. 19
  - SCENE III. The Duke of Albany's palace. 27
  - SCENE IV. A hall in the same. 29
  - SCENE V. Court before the same. 45
- **ACT 2** 48
  - SCENE I. Gloucester's castle. 49
  - SCENE II. Before Gloucester's castle. 55
  - SCENE III. A wood. 63
  - SCENE IV. Before Gloucester's castle. Kent in the stocks. 64
- **ACT 3** 78
  - SCENE I. A heath. 79
  - SCENE II. Another part of the heath. Storm still. 81
  - SCENE III. Gloucester's castle. 85
  - SCENE IV. The heath. Before a hovel. 87
  - SCENE V. Gloucester's castle. 96
  - SCENE VI. A chamber in a farmhouse adjoining the castle. 98
  - SCENE VII. Gloucester's castle. 104
- **ACT 4** 111
  - SCENE I. The heath. 112
  - SCENE II. Before Albany's palace. 116
  - SCENE III. The French camp near Dover. 121
  - SCENE IV. The same. A tent. 124
  - SCENE V. Gloucester's castle. 126
  - SCENE VI. Fields near Dover. 129
  - SCENE VII. A tent in the French camp. Lear on a bed asleep, ... 142
- **ACT 5** 147
  - SCENE I. The British camp, near Dover. 148
  - SCENE II. A field between the two camps. 152
  - SCENE III. The British camp near Dover. 153

About This Series

The "Classic Retold" series started as a way of telling classics for the modern reader—being careful to preserve the themes and integrity of the original. Whether you want to understand Shakespeare a little more or are trying to get a better grasps of the Greek classics, there is a book waiting for you!

The series is expanding every month. Visit BookCaps.com to see all the books in the series, and while you are there join the Facebook page, so you are first to know when a new book comes out.

Characters

Lear, King of Britain

King of France

Duke of Burgundy

Duke of Cornwall

Duke of Albany

Earl of Kent

Earl of Gloster

Edgar, Son to Gloster

Edmund, Bastard Son to Gloster

Curan, a Courtier

Old Man, Tenant to Gloster

Physician

Fool

Oswald, steward to Goneril

An Officer employed by Edmund

Gentleman, attendant on Cordelia

A Herald

Servants to Cornwall

Goneril, daughter to Lear

Regan, daughter to Lear

Cordelia, daughter to Lear

Knights attending on the King, Officers, Messengers, Soldiers, and Attendants.

Act 1

SCENE I. King Lear's palace.

Enter KENT, GLOUCESTER, and EDMUND

KENT
I thought the king had more affected the Duke of
Albany than Cornwall.

I thought the King preferred the Duke of Albany over Cornwall.

GLOUCESTER
It did always seem so to us: but now, in the division of the kingdom, it appears not which of the dukes he values most; for equalities are so weighed, that curiosity in neither can make choice
of either's moiety.

I always thought so too; but now, in the way he's split up the kingdom, one can't see which of the Dukes he prefers; it is so finely balanced that neither would be able to say that he prefers the other's portion.

KENT
Is not this your son, my lord?

Isn't this your son, my lord?

GLOUCESTER
His breeding, sir, hath been at my charge: I have so often blushed to acknowledge him, that now I am
brazed to it.

He was brought up, Sir, at my expense: I have so often been embarrassed to admit he's mine that now I'm quite hardened to it.

KENT
I cannot conceive you.

I can't make you out.

GLOUCESTER
Sir, this young fellow's mother could: whereupon
she grew round-wombed, and had, indeed, sir, a son
for her cradle ere she had a husband for her bed. Do you smell a fault?

Sir, this young fellow's mother could: and so her womb swelled and in fact she had a son in the cradle before she had a husband in her bed.
Do you think that's wrong?

KENT
I cannot wish the fault undone, the issue of it being so proper.

I wouldn't wish it any different, given there's such a good result.

GLOUCESTER
But I have, sir, a son by order of law, some year elder than this, who yet is no dearer in my account:

But I have, sir, a legitimate son, a year older than this one, whom I don't rate as more important:

7

though this knave came something saucily into the
world before he was sent for, yet was his mother fair; there was good sport at his making, and the whoreson must be acknowledged. Do you know this
noble gentleman, Edmund?

although this scoundrel came rather cheekily into
the world before he was wanted, his mother was beautiful; conceiving him was good fun, and the bastard must be acknowledged. Do you know this
noble gentleman, Edmund?

EDMUND
No, my lord.

No, my lord.

GLOUCESTER
My lord of Kent: remember him hereafter as my honourable friend.

The Earl of Kent: from now on always remember that he is my honored friend.

EDMUND
My services to your lordship.

At your Lordship's service.

KENT
I must love you, and sue to know you better.

We must be friends, and I will try to get to know you better.

EDMUND
Sir, I shall study deserving.

Sir, I shall try to deserve the compliment.

GLOUCESTER
He hath been out nine years, and away he shall again. The king is coming.

He's been abroad for nine years, and he'll be going back. The King is coming.

Sennet. Enter KING LEAR, CORNWALL, ALBANY, GONERIL, REGAN, CORDELIA, and Attendants

KING LEAR
Attend the lords of France and Burgundy, Gloucester.

Go and look after the lords of France and Burgundy, Gloucester.

GLOUCESTER
I shall, my liege.

I shall, my lord.

Exeunt GLOUCESTER and EDMUND

KING LEAR
Meantime we shall express our darker purpose. Give me the map there. Know that we have divided
In three our kingdom: and 'tis our fast intent

In the meantime I shall reveal my secret plan. Give me that map. Be aware that I have divided my kingdom into three: I am determined to throw off all work and duty in my old age;

To shake all cares and business from our age;
Conferring them on younger strengths, while we
Unburthen'd crawl toward death. Our son of
Cornwall,
And you, our no less loving son of Albany,
We have this hour a constant will to publish
Our daughters' several dowers, that future strife
May be prevented now. The princes, France and
Burgundy,
Great rivals in our youngest daughter's love,
Long in our court have made their amorous
sojourn,
And here are to be answer'd. Tell me, my
daughters,--
Since now we will divest us both of rule,
Interest of territory, cares of state,--
Which of you shall we say doth love us most?
That we our largest bounty may extend
Where nature doth with merit challenge.
Goneril,
Our eldest-born, speak first.

I will hand them over to younger men, while I crawl towards death unencumbered. Our son Cornwall,
and you, just as loving son Albany,
I have determined that today I will announce the different dowries of my daughters, so that we can nip any future disputes in the bud. The Princes of France and Burgundy,
great rivals for the love of my youngest daughter,
have been staying in my court, out of love, for a long time,
and will be given my decision today. Tell me, my daughters—
since I am now throwing off my kingship, ownership of land and the cares of state— which of you shall we say loves me the most? The biggest share will go to the one where merit most enhances nature. Goneril,
my firstborn, you speak first.

GONERIL
Sir, I love you more than words can wield the
matter;
Dearer than eye-sight, space, and liberty;
Beyond what can be valued, rich or rare;
No less than life, with grace, health, beauty,
honour;
As much as child e'er loved, or father found;
A love that makes breath poor, and speech
unable;
Beyond all manner of so much I love you.

Sir, I love you more than words can express; more than my eyesight, my freedom and my liberty;
more than anything of value, expensive or rare; as much as life, grace, health, beauty, honor;
I am the most loving child ever, no father could find better;
my love makes me breathless and speechless; I love you beyond all expression.

CORDELIA
[Aside] What shall Cordelia do?
Love, and be silent.

What shall Cordelia do?
You must love, and be silent.

LEAR
Of all these bounds, even from this line to this,
With shadowy forests and with champains
rich'd,
With plenteous rivers and wide-skirted meads,
We make thee lady: to thine and Albany's issue
Be this perpetual. What says our second
daughter,

All of this territory, from this line to this,
full of shady forests and open plains,
with many rivers and extensive meadows,
we make you the lady of: this shall be handed down to your children
in perpetuity. What does my second daughter say,

9

Our dearest Regan, wife to Cornwall? Speak.

REGAN
Sir, I am made
Of the self-same metal that my sister is,
And prize me at her worth. In my true heart
I find she names my very deed of love;
Only she comes too short: that I profess
Myself an enemy to all other joys,
Which the most precious square of sense possesses;
And find I am alone felicitate
In your dear highness' love.

CORDELIA
[Aside] Then poor Cordelia!
And yet not so; since, I am sure, my love's
More richer than my tongue.

KING LEAR
To thee and thine hereditary ever
Remain this ample third of our fair kingdom;
No less in space, validity, and pleasure,
Than that conferr'd on Goneril. Now, our joy,
Although the last, not least; to whose young love
The vines of France and milk of Burgundy
Strive to be interess'd; what can you say to draw
A third more opulent than your sisters? Speak.

CORDELIA
Nothing, my lord.

KING LEAR
Nothing!

CORDELIA
Nothing.

KING LEAR
Nothing will come of nothing: speak again.

CORDELIA
Unhappy that I am, I cannot heave
My heart into my mouth: I love your majesty

---

dearest Regan, the wife of Cornwall? Speak.

*Sir, I am
identical in this way to my sister,
and of equal merit. She has
spoken everything that is in my heart,
only she falls short: I have to say
that no other happiness means anything to me,
nothing which the highest sense could feel;
the only thing that makes me happy
is your dear highness' love.*

*This is bad for you Cordelia!
And yet it isn't, since I'm sure that my love
is more than I can say.*

*You and your descendants for ever
shall have this large third of my beautiful country;
it's no less spacious, profitable or lovely
than Goneril's share. Now, the light of my eye,
last but not least; the one whose young love
the Dukes of France and Burgundy
are fighting to win; what can you say to get
a richer third than your sisters? Speak.*

Nothing, my lord.

Nothing!

Nothing.

You won't get anything for nothing: try again.

*I'm sorry, but I cannot force myself
to express my feelings: I love your Majesty*

According to my bond; nor more nor less.

KING LEAR
How, how, Cordelia! mend your speech a little,
Lest it may mar your fortunes.

CORDELIA
Good my lord,
You have begot me, bred me, loved me: I
Return those duties back as are right fit,
Obey you, love you, and most honour you.
Why have my sisters husbands, if they say
They love you all? Haply, when I shall wed,
That lord whose hand must take my plight shall carry
Half my love with him, half my care and duty:
Sure, I shall never marry like my sisters,
To love my father all.

KING LEAR
But goes thy heart with this?

CORDELIA
Ay, good my lord.

KING LEAR
So young, and so untender?

CORDELIA
So young, my lord, and true.

KING LEAR
Let it be so; thy truth, then, be thy dower:
For, by the sacred radiance of the sun,
The mysteries of Hecate, and the night;
By all the operation of the orbs
From whom we do exist, and cease to be;
Here I disclaim all my paternal care,
Propinquity and property of blood,
And as a stranger to my heart and me
Hold thee, from this, for ever. The barbarous Scythian,
Or he that makes his generation messes
To gorge his appetite, shall to my bosom
Be as well neighbour'd, pitied, and relieved,
As thou my sometime daughter.

just as I should; no more nor less.

*What's this, Cordelia! You should speak differently,
or you'll talk yourself out of your fortune.*

*My good lord,
you've fathered me, brought me up and loved me: I repay you in the proper way,
by obeying you, loving you and honoring you.
Why do my sisters have husbands, if they say
that all their love is for you? When and if I marry,
the lord who takes my hand will also get
half my love, of my attention and care:
I certainly will not marry like my sisters,
only having love for my father.*

Are you speaking from the heart?

Yes, my good lord.

You're so young and so hardhearted?

So young, my lord, and honest.

*So be it; let your honesty be your dowry then:
by the holy light of the sun,
these secrets of the underworld and the night;
by the movement of the stars
which mark our births and deaths;
I hereby disown all my fatherly duties,
family relations and blood ties,
and declare that you are now a stranger to my
heart and me forever, from this moment on. The barbarian Scythian,
or the ones who make their parents into stews
to assuage their appetites, shall be as close
to my heart, just as helped and pitied
as you, who was once my daughter.*

KENT
Good my liege,-- | *My good Lord—*

KING LEAR
Peace, Kent!
Come not between the dragon and his wrath.
I loved her most, and thought to set my rest
On her kind nursery. Hence, and avoid my sight!
So be my grave my peace, as here I give
Her father's heart from her! Call France; who stirs?
Call Burgundy. Cornwall and Albany,
With my two daughters' dowers digest this third:
Let pride, which she calls plainness, marry her.
I do invest you jointly with my power,
Pre-eminence, and all the large effects
That troop with majesty. Ourself, by monthly course,
With reservation of an hundred knights,
By you to be sustain'd, shall our abode
Make with you by due turns. Only we still retain
The name, and all the additions to a king;
The sway, revenue, execution of the rest,
Beloved sons, be yours: which to confirm,
This coronet part betwixt you.

Quiet, Kent! Do not come between the Dragon and his victim. I loved her the most, and thought that she would look after me in my retirement. Get out, don't let me see you again! There will be no peace this side of the grave, and I take her father's heart away from her! Call France; who's going to do it? Call Burgundy. Cornwall and Albany, take this extra third along with my two daughters' dowries: let her marry her pride, which she calls honesty; I give you both my power to share, my superiority and all the other privileges of kingship. I shall stay with you month and month about with a retinue of a hundred knights, which you shall pay for. I shall keep the title of King, and the honours due to it; the power, income and administration of the rest is yours, beloved sons: to confirm this you can split this crown between you.

Giving the crown

KENT
Royal Lear,
Whom I have ever honour'd as my king,
Loved as my father, as my master follow'd,
As my great patron thought on in my prayers,--

Royal Lear, whom I have always honoured as my King, loved as my father, and followed as my master, remembered you in my prayers as my great patron—

KING LEAR
The bow is bent and drawn, make from the shaft. | *Enough preamble, make your point.*

KENT
Let it fall rather, though the fork invade
The region of my heart: be Kent unmannerly,
When Lear is mad. What wilt thou do, old man?
Think'st thou that duty shall have dread to speak,
When power to flattery bows? To plainness

I will make it, although the point might go through my heart: Kent will be discourteous, when Lear is mad. What are you doing, old man? Do you think that duty should be silent, when power gives in to flattery? Honor demands

honour's bound,
When majesty stoops to folly. Reverse thy doom;
And, in thy best consideration, cheque
This hideous rashness: answer my life my judgment,
Thy youngest daughter does not love thee least;
Nor are those empty-hearted whose low sound
Reverbs no hollowness.

KING LEAR
Kent, on thy life, no more.

KENT
My life I never held but as a pawn
To wage against thy enemies; nor fear to lose it,
Thy safety being the motive.

KING LEAR
Out of my sight!

KENT
See better, Lear; and let me still remain
The true blank of thine eye.

KING LEAR
Now, by Apollo,--

KENT
Now, by Apollo, king,
Thou swear'st thy gods in vain.

KING LEAR
O, vassal! miscreant!

Laying his hand on his sword

ALBANY CORNWALL
Dear sir, forbear.

KENT
Do:
Kill thy physician, and the fee bestow
Upon thy foul disease. Revoke thy doom;
Or, whilst I can vent clamour from my throat,
I'll tell thee thou dost evil.

honesty,
when royalty acts stupidly. Take back your pronouncement;
think more carefully and stop
this ghastly foolishness: I will stake my life on the fact
that your youngest daughter does not love you the least;
just because somebody is not shallow
it does not mean they are empty hearted.

Kent, if you value your life, be quiet.

I never thought of my life as anything but a pawn in the fight against your enemies: and I do not fear losing it if your safety is at stake.

Get out of my sight!

See more clearly, Lear; let me stay before you and advise you.

Now, by Apollo–

Now, by Apollo, King,
you're taking your god's name in vain.

Oh, you slave! Scoundrel!

Dear Sir, hold back.

Do:
kill your doctor, and give the fee
to your foul disease. Take back your pronouncement; or, as long as I can still speak, I'll tell you you're doing wrong.

KING LEAR
Hear me, recreant!
On thine allegiance, hear me!
Since thou hast sought to make us break our vow,
Which we durst never yet, and with strain'd pride
To come between our sentence and our power,
Which nor our nature nor our place can bear,
Our potency made good, take thy reward.
Five days we do allot thee, for provision
To shield thee from diseases of the world;
And on the sixth to turn thy hated back
Upon our kingdom: if, on the tenth day following,
Thy banish'd trunk be found in our dominions,
The moment is thy death. Away! by Jupiter,
This shall not be revoked.

Listen to me, you traitor!
Stick to your duty, listen to me!
Since you have tried to make me break my vow, which I have never done, and with unnatural pride
have tried to come between my decision and its execution,
which neither my nature nor my position can tolerate,
I will show my power, here is your reward.
I give you five days to prepare yourself against what the world may bring;
on the sixth you shall turn your hated back upon my kingdom: if, on the tenth day after that, your exiled body is found in my kingdom, you shall be executed. Get out! by Jupiter, I shall stick to this.

KENT
Fare thee well, king: sith thus thou wilt appear,
Freedom lives hence, and banishment is here.

Farewell, King: since you will behave like this, freedom lives elsewhere, and exile is here.

To CORDELIA
The gods to their dear shelter take thee, maid,
That justly think'st, and hast most rightly said!

Maiden, may the gods take you under their sweet protection, your thoughts are correct and you were right to speak out!

To REGAN and GONERIL
And your large speeches may your deeds approve,
That good effects may spring from words of love.
Thus Kent, O princes, bids you all adieu;
He'll shape his old course in a country new.

And may your deeds be as good as your great speeches,
so good things come from the words of love.
So, Princes, Kent says goodbye to all of you;
he'll follow his old ways in a new country.

Exit

Flourish. Re-enter GLOUCESTER, with KING OF FRANCE, BURGUNDY, and Attendants

GLOUCESTER
Here's France and Burgundy, my noble lord.

Here are France and Burgundy, my noble lord.

KING LEAR
My lord of Burgundy.

My lord of Burgundy,

We first address towards you, who with this king Hath rivall'd for our daughter: what, in the least, Will you require in present dower with her, Or cease your quest of love?	we will ask you first, who have been competing with this king for daughter: what is the smallest dowry you would accept with her, or withdraw your suit?

BURGUNDY

Most royal majesty, I crave no more than what your highness offer'd, Nor will you tender less.	Most royal majesty, I want no more than what your Highness offered, and you will not offer less.

KING LEAR

Right noble Burgundy, When she was dear to us, we did hold her so; But now her price is fall'n. Sir, there she stands: If aught within that little seeming substance, Or all of it, with our displeasure pieced, And nothing more, may fitly like your grace, She's there, and she is yours.	Truly noble Burgundy, when I loved her, I valued her at one price; but now her price has fallen. Sir, there she is: if there's anything in that insignificant thing, or all of it, with our displeasure attached to it, and nothing else, suits your Grace, there she is, and you can have her.

BURGUNDY

I know no answer.	I don't know what to say.

KING LEAR

Will you, with those infirmities she owes, Unfriended, new-adopted to our hate, Dower'd with our curse, and stranger'd with our oath, Take her, or leave her?	Will you, considering the weaknesses she has, friendless, newly hated by me, bringing my curse as her dowry, and exiled by my vow, take her or leave her?

BURGUNDY

Pardon me, royal sir; Election makes not up on such conditions.	Pardon me, your Highness; I can't choose under those conditions.

KING LEAR

Then leave her, sir; for, by the power that made me, I tell you all her wealth.	Then leave her, Sir; for I swear to God I have told you all she has.

To KING OF FRANCE

For you, great king, I would not from your love make such a stray, To match you where I hate; therefore beseech you To avert your liking a more worthier way Than on a wretch whom nature is ashamed	As for you, great King, I would not insult your love, by marrying you to someone I hated; so I ask you to look for someone better to love than a wretch whom nature

Almost to acknowledge hers. | has almost disowned.

KING OF FRANCE
This is most strange,
That she, that even but now was your best object,
The argument of your praise, balm of your age,
Most best, most dearest, should in this trice of time
Commit a thing so monstrous, to dismantle
So many folds of favour. Sure, her offence
Must be of such unnatural degree,
That monsters it, or your fore-vouch'd affection
Fall'n into taint: which to believe of her,
Must be a faith that reason without miracle
Could never plant in me.

*This is most odd,
that she, who just recently was your favourite thing,
the subject of all your praise, delight of your old age, best, dearest, should in the blink of an eye
do something so terrible that she would lose
all these marks of favour. The offence must surely
be so unnatural and monstrous
to pollute your former affection:
to believe that she could do something like that
is something that I could never do
without a miracle.*

CORDELIA
I yet beseech your majesty,--
If for I want that glib and oily art,
To speak and purpose not; since what I well intend,
I'll do't before I speak,--that you make known
It is no vicious blot, murder, or foulness,
No unchaste action, or dishonour'd step,
That hath deprived me of your grace and favour;
But even for want of that for which I am richer,
A still-soliciting eye, and such a tongue
As I am glad I have not, though not to have it
Hath lost me in your liking.

*Still I beg your Majesty's pardon,
if I am lacking in that shallow and oily skill,
to say things that I don't mean–what I do mean
I'll do before I speak of it–you must know
it is not some horrible character stain, murder or unpleasantness,
no unchaste behaviour, or dishonourable action,
that has taken your grace and favour away from me; what has is that I lack something which I am better for lacking, a beggar's eye, and a tongue that I am glad I have not got, even though not having it has cost me your approval.*

KING LEAR
Better thou
Hadst not been born than not to have pleased me better.

*It would have been better
for you never to have been born than not to be better at pleasing me.*

KING OF FRANCE
Is it but this,--a tardiness in nature
Which often leaves the history unspoke
That it intends to do? My lord of Burgundy,
What say you to the lady? Love's not love
When it is mingled with regards that stand
Aloof from the entire point. Will you have her?
She is herself a dowry.

*Is this all the problem–a natural reticence
which often doesn't speak
of what it intends to do? My lord of Burgundy,
what do you say to the lady? Love is not love
when it is mixed with desires that are
separate from the person. Will you have her?
She is enough, with or without dowry.*

BURGUNDY
Royal Lear,
Give but that portion which yourself proposed,
And here I take Cordelia by the hand,
Duchess of Burgundy.

Royal Lear, just give the share you mentioned and I will take Cordelia by the hand, and make her Duchess of Burgundy.

KING LEAR
Nothing: I have sworn; I am firm.

She will get nothing: I have sworn it; I won't be moved.

BURGUNDY
I am sorry, then, you have so lost a father
That you must lose a husband.

I'm sorry that you have alienated your father so much that you have lost a husband as well.

CORDELIA
Peace be with Burgundy!
Since that respects of fortune are his love,
I shall not be his wife.

May Burgundy be at peace! Since possessions are what he loves, I will not marry him.

KING OF FRANCE
Fairest Cordelia, that art most rich, being poor;
Most choice, forsaken; and most loved, despised!
Thee and thy virtues here I seize upon:
Be it lawful I take up what's cast away.
Gods, gods! 'tis strange that from their cold'st neglect
My love should kindle to inflamed respect.
Thy dowerless daughter, king, thrown to my chance,
Is queen of us, of ours, and our fair France:
Not all the dukes of waterish Burgundy
Can buy this unprized precious maid of me.
Bid them farewell, Cordelia, though unkind:
Thou losest here, a better where to find.

Fairest Cordelia, who is richest when poor; most wanted when abandoned; and most loved when despised! I will take you and your goodness: it's permitted for me to pick up what has been thrown away. By God! It is strange that their cold rejection has kindled my love and respect. King, your disinherited daughter, come to me by chance, is the queen of me, my people and my fair country, France: all the Dukes of weak Burgundy cannot buy this unvalued precious girl from me. Say goodbye to them, Cordelia, though they've treated you badly: you have lost this place, but you are going to a better one.

KING LEAR
Thou hast her, France: let her be thine; for we
Have no such daughter, nor shall ever see
That face of hers again. Therefore be gone
Without our grace, our love, our benison.
Come, noble Burgundy.

You have her, France: you can keep her; I have no daughter like her, and will never look on her face again. So get out, without my kindness, my love, or my blessing. Come on, noble Burgundy.

Flourish. Exeunt all but KING OF FRANCE, GONERIL, REGAN, and CORDELIA

KING OF FRANCE
Bid farewell to your sisters.

Say goodbye to your sisters.

CORDELIA
The jewels of our father, with wash'd eyes
Cordelia leaves you: I know you what you are;
And like a sister am most loath to call
Your faults as they are named. Use well our father:
To your professed bosoms I commit him
But yet, alas, stood I within his grace,
I would prefer him to a better place.
So, farewell to you both.

You, my father's treasures, Cordelia leaves you with eyes washed clean with tears: I know what you are;
and as your sister I am reluctant to specify your faults. Be good to our father: I hand him over to the love you spoke of, although, sadly, if he still liked me I would sooner he had better care.
So, farewell to you both.

REGAN
Prescribe not us our duties.

Don't tell us what to do.

GONERIL
Let your study
Be to content your lord, who hath received you
At fortune's alms. You have obedience scanted,
And well are worth the want that you have wanted.

You should be thinking about how to please your husband, who has accepted you as a beggar accepts money. You have lacked obedience, and deserve to be badly treated on account of it.

CORDELIA
Time shall unfold what plaited cunning hides:
Who cover faults, at last shame them derides.
Well may you prosper!

Time will reveal what twisted cunning has hidden: whoever hides their faults will get found out in the end. Good luck to you!

KING OF FRANCE
Come, my fair Cordelia.

Come with me, my fair Cordelia.

Exeunt KING OF FRANCE and CORDELIA

GONERIL
Sister, it is not a little I have to say of what most nearly appertains to us both. I think our father will hence to-night.

Sister, I have much to say about matters which closely concern us both. I think our father will leave here tonight.

REGAN
That's most certain, and with you; next month with us.

Definitely, he'll go with you; next month he'll come to me.

GONERIL
You see how full of changes his age is; the observation we have made of it hath not been little: he always loved our sister most; and with what poor judgment he hath now cast her

You see how much his age has changed him; I have seen plenty of evidence: he always loved our sister the best, and in his rejection of her his poor judgement

18

off
appears too grossly.

REGAN
'Tis the infirmity of his age: yet he hath ever but slenderly known himself.

GONERIL
The best and soundest of his time hath been but rash; then must we look to receive from his age, not alone the imperfections of long-engraffed condition, but therewithal the unruly waywardness
that infirm and choleric years bring with them.

REGAN
Such unconstant starts are we like to have from him as this of Kent's banishment.

GONERIL
There is further compliment of leavetaking between France and him. Pray you, let's hit together: if our father carry authority with such dispositions as he bears, this last surrender of his will but offend us.

REGAN
We shall further think on't.

GONERIL
We must do something, and i' the heat.

Exeunt

---

is all too obvious.

It's part of the weakness of age, though he's always been unthinking.

Even when he was in the peak of condition he was hotheaded; and so as he gets older we must expect not only to have to put up with his firmly embedded temper, but along with it the chaotic changeability
that his old age and illness will bring with them.

We will have to expect sudden whims from him like this exiling of Kent.

There are going to be more formal goodbyes between him and France. Come on, let's stick together: if our father is going to exercise his power with these sort of moods his recent arrangements will be a nuisance to us.

I shall think more about it.

We must do something, and do it quickly.

SCENE II. The Earl of Gloucester's castle.

Enter EDMUND, with a letter

EDMUND
Thou, nature, art my goddess; to thy law
My services are bound. Wherefore should I
Stand in the plague of custom, and permit
The curiosity of nations to deprive me,
For that I am some twelve or fourteen moon-shines
Lag of a brother? Why bastard? wherefore base?
When my dimensions are as well compact,
My mind as generous, and my shape as true,
As honest madam's issue? Why brand they us
With base? with baseness? bastardy? base, base?
Who, in the lusty stealth of nature, take
More composition and fierce quality
Than doth, within a dull, stale, tired bed,
Go to the creating a whole tribe of fops,
Got 'tween asleep and wake? Well, then,
Legitimate Edgar, I must have your land:
Our father's love is to the bastard Edmund
As to the legitimate: fine word,--legitimate!
Well, my legitimate, if this letter speed,
And my invention thrive, Edmund the base
Shall top the legitimate. I grow; I prosper:
Now, gods, stand up for bastards!

You, nature, are my Goddess; I am a servant of your laws. Why should I have to suffer from tradition, and allow squeamish customs to keep me deprived, just because I am twelve or fourteen months younger than my brother? Why am I called a bastard? Why am I thought lowly? I have just as good a body, my mind is just as noble, I look just as much like my father as the child of a married woman. Why do they brand me as lowly? Having low nature? Bastardy? Low, low? I, from those lusty natural acts, get a more rounded nature and greater energy than you get from creating a whole tribe of weaklings in a dull, stale, tired bed, conceived by half asleep lovers. So then, Edgar the legitimate, I must have your land: our father loves the bastard Edmund just as much as the legitimate son: that's a good word, legitimate! Well, legitimate one, if this letter does well, and my plans thrive, Edmund the bastard will beat the legitimate. I am growing: I shall prosper: now, gods, stand up for bastards!

Enter GLOUCESTER

GLOUCESTER
Kent banish'd thus! and France in choler parted!
And the king gone to-night! subscribed his power!
Confined to exhibition! All this done
Upon the gad! Edmund, how now! what news?

Kent exiled like this! And France gone off in anger! And the King going tonight! He's handed over his power! Restricted himself to an allowance! And all this done on the spur of the moment! Edmund, what's up! What's the news?

EDMUND
So please your lordship, none.

None, my good lord.

Putting up the letter

GLOUCESTER
Why so earnestly seek you to put up that letter?

Why are you trying so hard to hide that letter?

EDMUND
I know no news, my lord.

I have no news, my lord.

GLOUCESTER
What paper were you reading?

What was that letter you were reading?

EDMUND
Nothing, my lord.

Nothing, my lord.

GLOUCESTER
No? What needed, then, that terrible dispatch of it into your pocket? the quality of nothing hath not such need to hide itself. Let's see: come, if it be nothing, I shall not need spectacles.

Nothing? Then why did you need to put it in your pocket so hurriedly? If it is nothing then you have nothing to hide. Show me: come on, if it's nothing, I shan't need my glasses.

EDMUND
I beseech you, sir, pardon me: it is a letter from my brother, that I have not all o'er-read; and for so much as I have perused, I find it not fit for your o'er-looking.

I beg you, sir, not too ask me: it is a letter from my brother, and I have not read it fully; as for the bit which I have read, I do not think it's suitable for you.

GLOUCESTER
Give me the letter, sir.

Give it to me, sir.

EDMUND
I shall offend, either to detain or give it. The contents, as in part I understand them, are to blame.

I will offend you whether I refuse or hand it over. That's the fault of its content, as far as I understand it.

GLOUCESTER
Let's see, let's see.

Come on, show me.

EDMUND
I hope, for my brother's justification, he wrote this but as an essay or taste of my virtue.

I hope, for my brother's sake, that he wrote this just to make a test of my loyalty.

GLOUCESTER
[Reads] 'This policy and reverence of age makes the world bitter to the best of our times; keeps our fortunes from us till our oldness cannot relish
them. I begin to find an idle and fond bondage in the oppression of aged tyranny; who sways, not
as it hath power, but as it is suffered. Come to me, that of this I may speak more. If our father

*'This tradition of favouring the old makes the world a worse place for the best men of the time;
it keeps our fortune from us until we are too old to enjoy it. I am beginning to think that the oppression of
that old tyrant is useless and stupid slavery; he only
has power because we put up with him. Come*

would sleep till I waked him, you should half his revenue for ever, and live the beloved of your brother, EDGAR.'
Hum--conspiracy!--'Sleep till I waked him,--you should enjoy half his revenue,'--My son Edgar! Had he a hand to write this? a heart and brain to breed it in?--When came this to you? who brought it?

EDMUND
It was not brought me, my lord; there's the cunning of it; I found it thrown in at the casement of my closet.

GLOUCESTER
You know the character to be your brother's?

EDMUND
If the matter were good, my lord, I durst swear it were his; but, in respect of that, I would fain think it were not.

GLOUCESTER
It is his.

EDMUND
It is his hand, my lord; but I hope his heart is not in the contents.

GLOUCESTER
Hath he never heretofore sounded you in this business?

EDMUND
Never, my lord: but I have heard him oft maintain it to be fit, that, sons at perfect age, and fathers declining, the father should be as ward to the son, and the son manage his revenue.

GLOUCESTER
O villain, villain! His very opinion in the letter! Abhorred villain! Unnatural, detested, brutish villain! worse than brutish! Go, sirrah, seek him; I'll apprehend him: abominable

and see me so I can say more about this. If our father could be put to sleep, you would have half of his income for ever, and be greatly loved by your brother, Edgar.' Hmm, conspiracy! 'Put to sleep–you will have half of his income,'–my son Edgar! Did he write this with his own hand? Did he think and feel this? How did you get this? Who brought it?

Nobody gave it to me, my lord; there's the deviousness of it; it was thrown in through my bedroom window.

Do you recognise your brother's handwriting?

If the subject was good, my lord, I would swear that it was; but given the subject matter I would rather believe that it is not.

It is his.

It is his handwriting, my lord; but I hope the contents do not reflect his heart.

Has he never sounded you out about this sort of thing before?

Never, my lord: but I've often heard him say that it is right, when sons are in their prime and fathers getting old, that the father should be obedient to the son, and the son should manage his income.

Oh, the scoundrel! This is just what he says in the letter! Disgusting scoundrel! Unnatural, hated, brutal scoundrel! Worse than brutal! Go, sir,

22

villain!
Where is he?

EDMUND
I do not well know, my lord. If it shall please you to suspend your indignation against my brother till you can derive from him better testimony of his intent, you shall run a certain course; where, if you violently proceed against him, mistaking his purpose, it would make a great
gap in your own honour, and shake in pieces the heart of his obedience. I dare pawn down my life
for him, that he hath wrote this to feel my affection to your honour, and to no further pretence of danger.

GLOUCESTER
Think you so?

EDMUND
If your honour judge it meet, I will place you where you shall hear us confer of this, and by an auricular assurance have your satisfaction; and that without any further delay than this very evening.

GLOUCESTER
He cannot be such a monster--

EDMUND
Nor is not, sure.

GLOUCESTER
To his father, that so tenderly and entirely loves him. Heaven and earth! Edmund, seek him out: wind me into him, I pray you: frame the business after your own wisdom. I would unstate
myself, to be in a due resolution.

EDMUND
I will seek him, sir, presently: convey the business as I shall find means and acquaint you withal.

---

find him; I'll question him: terrible scoundrel! Where is he?

I'm not sure, my lord. It would be best for you to hold back your anger against my brother until you can get a better idea of what he means; if you rush to judge him, misunderstanding what he means, it would be a great stain on your own honour, and it would destroy his loyalty. I would bet my life that he wrote this to test my loyalty to you, and that's all there is to it.

Do you think so?

If your honour thinks it appropriate, I will hide you somewhere where you can hear us talk about this, and you shall be reassured by the proof you hear; we'll do this this evening at the latest.

He can't be such a monster--

I'm sure he's not.

To his father, who gives him such tender and complete love. Good heavens! Edmund, find him: worm your way into his confidence for me, please: do it in whatever ways seems best to you. I would give up everything to get to the bottom of this.

I will look for him, sir, shortly: I'll carry it out in whatever way appears best and let you know at once.

GLOUCESTER
These late eclipses in the sun and moon portend no good to us: though the wisdom of nature can reason it thus and thus, yet nature finds itself scourged by the sequent effects: love cools, friendship falls off, brothers divide: in cities, mutinies; in countries, discord; in palaces, treason; and the bond cracked 'twixt son and father. This villain of mine comes under the prediction; there's son against father: the king falls from bias of nature; there's father against child. We have seen the best of our time: machinations, hollowness, treachery, and all ruinous disorders, follow us disquietly to our graves. Find out this villain, Edmund; it shall lose thee nothing; do it carefully. And the noble and true-hearted Kent banished! his offence, honesty! 'Tis strange.

These recent eclipses of the sun and moon mean us no good: although science can say it has reasons for it, nature itself suffers the after-effects: love cools, friendship fades, brothers fight: there are rebellions in the cities; countries are unsettled; there is treason in palaces; and the bond between a son and his father is broken. My villainous son fits into this; the son who's going against his father: the King has fallen from his natural place; a father has fallen out with his child. We are past the good times now: plotting, falseness, treachery, and all other terrible disruptions, will follow us unhappily to our graves. Uncover this villain, Edmund; you won't be the loser by it; do it carefully. And the noble and loyal Kent has been exiled, for being honest! It's strange.

Exit

EDMUND
This is the excellent foppery of the world, that, when we are sick in fortune,--often the surfeit of our own behavior,--we make guilty of our disasters the sun, the moon, and the stars: as if we were villains by necessity; fools by heavenly compulsion; knaves, thieves, and treachers, by spherical predominance; drunkards, liars, and adulterers, by an enforced obedience of planetary influence; and all that we are evil in, by a divine thrusting on: an admirable evasion of whoremaster man, to lay his goatish disposition to the charge of a star! My father compounded with my mother under the dragon's tail; and my nativity was under Ursa major; so that it follows, I am rough and lecherous. Tut, I should have been that I am, had the maidenliest star in the firmament twinkled on my bastardizing. Edgar--

This is the great stupidity of the world, that, when things go against us--often due to our own behaviour--we blame the sun, the moon, and the stars for disasters: as if we were forced to be villains; the heavens made us fools; the stars forced us to be knaves, thieves and traitors; we are only drunkards, liars, and adulterers because of the influence of the planets; and we blame everything we do wrong on the influence of heaven: what a great excuse for these sluttish men, to blame their randy nature on the stars! My father mated with my mother under the sign of the Dragon, and I was born under Ursa major; so it follows that I must be rough and lecherous. What nonsense, I would have been the person I am, if the most chaste star in the sky had shone on my bastard conception.

Enter EDGAR
And pat he comes like the catastrophe of the old

And here he comes, like the denouement of an

24

comedy: my cue is villanous melancholy, with a sigh like Tom o' Bedlam. O, these eclipses do portend these divisions! fa, sol, la, mi.

EDGAR
How now, brother Edmund! what serious contemplation are you in?

EDMUND
I am thinking, brother, of a prediction I read this other day, what should follow these eclipses.

EDGAR
Do you busy yourself about that?

EDMUND
I promise you, the effects he writes of succeed unhappily; as of unnaturalness between the child and the parent; death, dearth, dissolutions of ancient amities; divisions in state, menaces and maledictions against king and nobles; needless diffidences, banishment of friends, dissipation of cohorts, nuptial breaches, and I know not what.

EDGAR
How long have you been a sectary astronomical?

EDMUND
Come, come; when saw you my father last?

EDGAR
Why, the night gone by.

EDMUND
Spake you with him?

EDGAR
Ay, two hours together.

EDMUND
Parted you in good terms? Found you no displeasure in him by word or countenance?

---

old comedy, I shall look deeply sad, sighing like a mad beggar. Oh! How the eclipses signal divisions! Tra la, tra la...

Hello there, brother Edmund! What are you thinking about so seriously?

I'm thinking, brother, of a horoscope I read the other day saying what effects these eclipses would have.

Are you wasting your time with that?

I can assure you that unfortunately the consequences he writes of are happening; such as separations between children and parents; death, famine, the breaking of ancient alliances; splits in government, threats and curses against the King and nobility; baseless suspicions, the exile of friends, desertion of soldiers, breaking of marriages, and heaven knows what else.

How long have you been an astrologer?

Never mind that; when did you last see my father?

Why, last night.

Did you speak with him?

Yes, for a whole two hours.

Did you part on good terms? Didn't you notice anything in his words or appearance that showed displeasure?

EDGAR
None at all.

Nothing at all.

EDMUND
Bethink yourself wherein you may have offended
him: and at my entreaty forbear his presence
till some little time hath qualified the heat of
his displeasure; which at this instant so rageth
in him, that with the mischief of your person it
would scarcely allay.

*Try and think how you might have offended him;
take my advice, steer clear of him until
time has cooled his anger;
at the moment he is so boiling with it
that he would hardly be able to keep his hands
off you.*

EDGAR
Some villain hath done me wrong.

Some villain has been speaking against me.

EDMUND
That's my fear. I pray you, have a continent
forbearance till the spied of his rage goes
slower; and, as I say, retire with me to my
lodging, from whence I will fitly bring you to
hear my lord speak: pray ye, go; there's my key:
if you do stir abroad, go armed.

*That's what I'm worried about. I'm begging you
to be patient until he calms down;
and I advise you to come with me to my
lodgings, and I'll bring you to talk to him
when the time is right: go on, I'm telling you;
here's my key: if you do go out, go armed.*

EDGAR
Armed, brother!

Armed, brother!

EDMUND
Brother, I advise you to the best; go armed: I
am no honest man if there be any good meaning
towards you: I have told you what I have seen
and heard; but faintly, nothing like the image
and horror of it: pray you, away.

*Brother, I'm telling you for the best, go armed:
I would be lying if I said that things were all
right;
I have told you what I have seen and heard, but
I've just given you an outline, nothing like
the horrible reality: off you go, please.*

EDGAR
Shall I hear from you anon?

Will I hear from you soon?

EDMUND
I do serve you in this business.

I'm at your service.

Exit EDGAR
A credulous father! and a brother noble,
Whose nature is so far from doing harms,
That he suspects none: on whose foolish honesty
My practises ride easy! I see the business.
Let me, if not by birth, have lands by wit:

*A gullible father! And a noble brother, whose
nature is so good he does not suspect evil in
others: his foolish honesty helps my plots! I can
see the way forward. If I can't have lands as a
birthright, let me get them through cunning:*

26

All with me's meet that I can fashion fit. *for me the end justifies the means*.

SCENE III. The Duke of Albany's palace.

Enter GONERIL, and OSWALD, her steward

GONERIL
Did my father strike my gentleman for chiding
of his fool?

	Did my father hit my servant for criticising his fool?

OSWALD
Yes, madam.

Yes, madam.

GONERIL
By day and night he wrongs me; every hour
He flashes into one gross crime or other,
That sets us all at odds: I'll not endure it:
His knights grow riotous, and himself upbraids us
On every trifle. When he returns from hunting,
I will not speak with him; say I am sick:
If you come slack of former services,
You shall do well; the fault of it I'll answer.

He does me wrong day and night; not an hour goes by without some sort of explosion from him that upsets everything: I won't put up with it: his knights are rowdy, and he criticises me for every little thing. When he comes back from hunting I will not speak to him; say I am ill: I will be pleased if you show him less courtesy than you used to; I'll defend you.

OSWALD
He's coming, madam; I hear him.

He's coming, madam; I can hear him.

Horns within

GONERIL
Put on what weary negligence you please,
You and your fellows; I'll have it come to question:
If he dislike it, let him to our sister,
Whose mind and mine, I know, in that are one,
Not to be over-ruled. Idle old man,
That still would manage those authorities
That he hath given away! Now, by my life,
Old fools are babes again; and must be used
With cheques as flatteries,--when they are seen abused.
Remember what I tell you.

You and your comrades should be as lazy and negligent towards him as you like, I want it to come to a head: if he doesn't like it, let him go to my sister, who I know shares my feeling that we won't be bossed by him. Lazy old man, who still wants to use the power that he has given away! I swear, old fools go back to being babies; they have to be disciplined as well as comforted, when they misbehave. Remember what I say.

OSWALD
Well, madam.

Very good, madam.

GONERIL

And let his knights have colder looks among you;
What grows of it, no matter; advise your fellows so:
I would breed from hence occasions, and I shall,
That I may speak: I'll write straight to my sister,
To hold my very course. Prepare for dinner.

*And give his knights the cold shoulder;
don't worry about the outcome; tell your
comrades to do the same:
I want to use these things to my advantage,
giving me a chance to speak out: I'll write to my sister at once
to tell her to do the same. Get dinner ready.*

Exeunt

SCENE IV. A hall in the same.

Enter KENT, disguised

KENT
If but as well I other accents borrow,
That can my speech defuse, my good intent
May carry through itself to that full issue
For which I razed my likeness. Now, banish'd Kent,
If thou canst serve where thou dost stand condemn'd,
So may it come, thy master, whom thou lovest,
Shall find thee full of labours.

If I use other accents as well, to disguise my speech, my plans, for which I shaved my beard, may come to fruition. Now, exiled Kent, if you can give service to the one who condemned you it may turn out that your master, whom you love, will find your labours useful.

Horns within. Enter KING LEAR, Knights, and Attendants

KING LEAR
Let me not stay a jot for dinner; go get it ready.

Don't keep me waiting for my dinner; go and get it ready.

Exit an Attendant

How now! what art thou?

Hello! Who are you?

KENT
A man, sir.

A man, sir.

KING LEAR
What dost thou profess? what wouldst thou with us?

What's your trade, what do you want with me?

KENT
I do profess to be no less than I seem; to serve him truly that will put me in trust: to love him that is honest; to converse with him that is wise, and says little; to fear judgment; to fight when I cannot choose; and to eat no fish.

My trade is to be just who I am; to serve loyally someone who trusts me: to love someone who is honest; to talk with someone who is wise and says little; to fear judgement; to fight when I have to; and to be strong.

KING LEAR
What art thou?

Who are you?

KENT
A very honest-hearted fellow, and as poor as the king.

A man with a good heart, as poor as the King.

30

KING LEAR
If thou be as poor for a subject as he is for a king, thou art poor enough. What wouldst thou?

If your poverty as a subject is comparable to his poverty as a king, you are poor enough. What do you want?

KENT
Service.

To serve.

KING LEAR
Who wouldst thou serve?

Who do you want to serve?

KENT
You.

You.

KING LEAR
Dost thou know me, fellow?

Do you know who I am, fellow?

KENT
No, sir; but you have that in your countenance which I would fain call master.

No, sir; but there is something in your face which makes me want to call you my master.

KING LEAR
What's that?

What is it?

KENT
Authority.

Authority.

KING LEAR
What services canst thou do?

What services can you offer?

KENT
I can keep honest counsel, ride, run, mar a curious
tale in telling it, and deliver a plain message bluntly: that which ordinary men are fit for, I am qualified in; and the best of me is diligence.

I can keep a secret, ride, run errands, decipher mysteries, and deliver a simple message clearly; I'm good for anything ordinary men can do, and my best quality is that I'm a hard worker.

KING LEAR
How old art thou?

How old are you?

KENT
Not so young, sir, to love a woman for singing, nor
so old to dote on her for any thing: I have years on my back forty eight.

*I am not so young, sir, that I would love a woman for singing,
nor am I so old that I would drool over her: in terms of years I am forty-eight.*

KING LEAR

31

Follow me; thou shalt serve me: if I like thee no worse after dinner, I will not part from thee yet. Dinner, ho, dinner! Where's my knave? my fool? Go you, and call my fool hither.	*Come with me; you shall serve me: if I still like you after dinner, you can stay. Dinner, aha, dinner! Where's my knave? My fool?* *You, go and call my fool here.*

Exit an Attendant
Enter OSWALD

You, you, sirrah, where's my daughter?	*You there, where is my daughter?*

OSWALD
So please you,--	*If you'll excuse me–*

Exit

KING LEAR
What says the fellow there? Call the clotpoll back.	*What does that chap say? Call the blockhead back.*

Exit a Knight
Where's my fool, ho? I think the world's asleep.	*Where's my fool, eh? I think the whole world has gone to sleep.*

Re-enter Knight
How now! where's that mongrel?	*Now then! Where's that mongrel?*

Knight
He says, my lord, your daughter is not well.	*He says, my lord, that your daughter is ill.*

KING LEAR
Why came not the slave back to me when I called him?	*Why didn't the slave come back to me when I called?*

Knight
Sir, he answered me in the roundest manner, he would not.	*Sir, he answered me in the rudest possible way, saying he would not.*

KING LEAR
He would not!	*He would not!*

Knight
My lord, I know not what the matter is; but, to my judgment, your highness is not entertained with	*My lord, I don't know what's going on; but as far* *as I can see, your Highness is not welcomed*

that ceremonious affection as you were wont; there's a
great abatement of kindness appears as well in the
general dependants as in the duke himself also and
your daughter.

KING LEAR
Ha! sayest thou so?

Knight
I beseech you, pardon me, my lord, if I be mistaken;
for my duty cannot be silent when I think your highness wronged.

KING LEAR
Thou but rememberest me of mine own conception: I
have perceived a most faint neglect of late; which I
have rather blamed as mine own jealous curiosity
than as a very pretence and purpose of unkindness:
I will look further into't. But where's my fool? I have not seen him this two days.

Knight
Since my young lady's going into France, sir, the
fool hath much pined away.

KING LEAR
No more of that; I have noted it well. Go you, and
tell my daughter I would speak with her.

Exit an Attendant
Go you, call hither my fool.

Exit an Attendant

Re-enter OSWALD

---

with the same respectful affection as in the past; all the servants of the Duke seem to be disrespectful and so does he himself and your daughter.

Ha! You don't say?

I beg you to forgive me my lord, if I'm mistaken; my duty won't allow me to keep quiet when I think you are wronged.

You are just reminding me of my own suspicions: I have recently noticed them being a little neglectful; I thought that this was just my easily offended imagination, not deliberate: I'll investigate this further. But where is my fool? I haven't seen him for two days.

Since my young lady went to France, sir, the fool has been very depressed.

You don't need to tell me, I have noticed it. You, go and tell my daughter I want to speak with her.

And you, go and call my fool here.

O, you sir, you, come you hither, sir: who am I, sir?

OSWALD
My lady's father.

KING LEAR
'My lady's father'! my lord's knave: your whoreson dog! you slave! you cur!

OSWALD
I am none of these, my lord; I beseech your pardon.

KING LEAR
Do you bandy looks with me, you rascal?

Striking him

OSWALD
I'll not be struck, my lord.

KENT
Nor tripped neither, you base football player.

Tripping up his heels

KING LEAR
I thank thee, fellow; thou servest me, and I'll love thee.

KENT
Come, sir, arise, away! I'll teach you differences:
away, away! if you will measure your lubber's length again, tarry: but away! go to; have you wisdom? so.

Pushes OSWALD out

KING LEAR
Now, my friendly knave, I thank thee: there's earnest of thy service.

Giving KENT money

You, you sir, come here, sir: who am I, sir?

You are my lady's father.

'My lady's father'! My Lord's knave: you bastard dog! You slave! You dog!

I am none of these, my lord; please excuse me.

Will you exchange stares with me, you rascal?

You will not hit me, my lord.

We won't trip you up either, you lowlife footballer.

Thank you, my boy; you can serve me, and I will love you.

*Come on sir, get up and get out! I'll teach you to show disrespect! If you want to be knocked down
again, hang around: get lost! Get out; do you know what's good for you? Right.*

Now, my friendly knave, I thank you: here's a reward for your service.

34

Enter Fool

Fool
Let me hire him too: here's my coxcomb.

Offering KENT his cap

KING LEAR
How now, my pretty knave! how dost thou?

Fool
Sirrah, you were best take my coxcomb.

KENT
Why, fool?

Fool
Why, for taking one's part that's out of favour:
nay, an thou canst not smile as the wind sits,
thou'lt catch cold shortly: there, take my coxcomb:
why, this fellow has banished two on's daughters,
and did the third a blessing against his will; if thou follow him, thou must needs wear my coxcomb.
How now, nuncle! Would I had two coxcombs and two daughters!

KING LEAR
Why, my boy?

Fool
If I gave them all my living, I'd keep my coxcombs
myself. There's mine; beg another of thy daughters.

KING LEAR
Take heed, sirrah; the whip.

Fool
Truth's a dog must to kennel; he must be whipped
out, when Lady the brach may stand by the fire and stink.

Let me hire him too: here's my coxcomb.	*Let me hire him too: here's my jester's cap.*
How now, my pretty knave! how dost thou?	*Aha, my pretty knave! How are you?*
Sirrah, you were best take my coxcomb.	*Sir, you had better take my jester's hat.*
Why, fool?	*Why, fool?*
Why, for taking one's part...	*Why, for taking the side of someone who is out of favor: if you can't see which way the wind blows, you'll catch a cold shortly: so, take my jester's hat: this fellow has given freedom to two of his daughters, and done the third a good turn without meaning to; if you follow him, you need my jester's hat. How are you then, nuncle? I wish I had two hats and two daughters!*
Why, my boy?	*Why, my boy?*
If I gave them all my living...	*If I gave them my whole fortune, I would keep my fool's hats for myself. Here is mine; ask your daughters for another one.*
Take heed, sirrah; the whip.	*Be careful, sir; remember the whip.*
Truth's a dog must to kennel...	*Truth's a dog who must be contained; he must be whipped, when the bitch can stand by the fire and stink.*

KING LEAR
A pestilent gall to me!

You annoy me!

Fool
Sirrah, I'll teach thee a speech.

Sir, I'll teach you a speech.

KING LEAR
Do.

Do so.

Fool
Mark it, nuncle:
Have more than thou showest,
Speak less than thou knowest,
Lend less than thou owest,
Ride more than thou goest,
Learn more than thou trowest,
Set less than thou throwest;
Leave thy drink and thy whore,
And keep in-a-door,
And thou shalt have more
Than two tens to a score.

Make a note of it, nuncle:
have more than you show,
speak less than you know,
lend less than you owe,
ride more than you walk,
learn more than you guess,
don't gamble everything,
leave your drink and your whore,
keep indoors,
and you shall have more
than twenty shillings in your pound.

KENT
This is nothing, fool.

This means nothing, fool.

Fool
Then 'tis like the breath of an unfee'd lawyer; you
gave me nothing for't. Can you make no use of nothing, nuncle?

Then it's like the breath of an unpaid lawyer; you
didn't give me anything for it. Have you no use for nothing, nuncle?

KING LEAR
Why, no, boy; nothing can be made out of nothing.

Why, no, boy; you can't make anything from nothing.

Fool
[To KENT] Prithee, tell him, so much the rent of
his land comes to: he will not believe a fool.

Please, tell him, that's what the rent for his land is worth: he won't believe a fool.

KING LEAR
A bitter fool!

You're a sarcastic fool!

Fool
Dost thou know the difference, my boy, between

Do you know the difference, my boy, between

a bitter fool and a sweet fool?

KING LEAR
No, lad; teach me.

Fool
That lord that counsell'd thee
To give away thy land,
Come place him here by me,
Do thou for him stand:
The sweet and bitter fool
Will presently appear;
The one in motley here,
The other found out there.

KING LEAR
Dost thou call me fool, boy?

Fool
All thy other titles thou hast given away; that thou wast born with.

KENT
This is not altogether fool, my lord.

Fool
No, faith, lords and great men will not let me; if I had a monopoly out, they would have part on't: and ladies too, they will not let me have all fool to myself; they'll be snatching. Give me an egg, nuncle, and I'll give thee two crowns.

KING LEAR
What two crowns shall they be?

Fool
Why, after I have cut the egg i' the middle, and eat
up the meat, the two crowns of the egg. When thou
clovest thy crown i' the middle, and gavest away both parts, thou borest thy ass on thy back o'er the dirt: thou hadst little wit in thy bald crown, when thou gavest thy golden one away. If I speak
like myself in this, let him be whipped that first

a bitter fool and a sweet fool?

No, lad; teach me.

*The lord who advised you
to give away your land,
come and put him next to me,
you stand in for him:
in a moment you will see
the sweet and the bitter fool;
I am here in uniform,
and there's the other one.*

Are you calling me a fool, boy?

You've given away all your other titles; that one you were born with.

This is not a complete fool, my lord.

No, by God, lords and great men will not let me have it all; if I had a monopoly on foolishness, they would insist on a share: and the ladies too, they will not let me have all the foolishness for myself; they would snatch some. Give me an egg, nuncle, and I'll give you two crowns.

And what two crowns are those?

*Why, after I have cut the egg in half, and eaten the contents, you shall have the crowns of the shell.
When you cut your crown in half, and gave away both halves, you carried your ass on your back over the dirt: there wasn't much sense in your bald crown when you gave your golden one away. If I
am speaking like a fool, let the first one who sees*

37

finds it so.

Singing
Fools had ne'er less wit in a year;
For wise men are grown foppish,
They know not how their wits to wear,
Their manners are so apish.

KING LEAR
When were you wont to be so full of songs, sirrah?

Fool
I have used it, nuncle, ever since thou madest thy
daughters thy mothers: for when thou gavest them
the rod, and put'st down thine own breeches,

Singing
Then they for sudden joy did weep,
And I for sorrow sung,
That such a king should play bo-peep,
And go the fools among.
Prithee, nuncle, keep a schoolmaster that can teach
thy fool to lie: I would fain learn to lie.

KING LEAR
An you lie, sirrah, we'll have you whipped.

Fool
I marvel what kin thou and thy daughters are:
they'll have me whipped for speaking true, thou'lt
have me whipped for lying; and sometimes I am
whipped for holding my peace. I had rather be any
kind o' thing than a fool: and yet I would not be
thee, nuncle; thou hast pared thy wit o' both sides,
and left nothing i' the middle: here comes one o' the parings.

Enter GONERIL

---

it's true be whipped.

Fools were never so little needed as now when wise men have grown so foolish, they don't know how to use their wits, they're more like apes than anything.

Since when were you so full of songs, sir?

Ever since, nuncle, you made your daughters your mothers: you gave them the cane, and pulled down your pants,

Then they suddenly wept for joy, and I sang out of sadness, to see such a great king playing hide and seek amongst the fools.
Please, uncle, employ a schoolmaster that can teach your fool to lie: I would like to learn to lie.

If you lie, sir, we'll have you whipped.

It's amazing that you and your daughters are related:
they want to whip me for telling the truth, you for lying; and sometimes I am whipped for keeping quiet. I'd rather be anything but a fool: and yet I would not want to be you, nuncle; you have shaved your sense on both sides and left nothing in the middle: here comes one of the shavings.

KING LEAR
How now, daughter! what makes that frontlet on?
Methinks you are too much of late i' the frown.

Fool
Thou wast a pretty fellow when thou hadst no need to
care for her frowning; now thou art an O without a
figure: I am better than thou art now; I am a fool,
thou art nothing.

To GONERIL
Yes, forsooth, I will hold my tongue; so your face
bids me, though you say nothing. Mum, mum,
He that keeps nor crust nor crum,
Weary of all, shall want some.

Pointing to KING LEAR
That's a shealed peascod.

GONERIL
Not only, sir, this your all-licensed fool,
But other of your insolent retinue
Do hourly carp and quarrel; breaking forth
In rank and not-to-be endured riots. Sir,
I had thought, by making this well known unto you,
To have found a safe redress; but now grow fearful,
By what yourself too late have spoke and done.
That you protect this course, and put it on
By your allowance; which if you should, the fault
Would not 'scape censure, nor the redresses sleep,
Which, in the tender of a wholesome weal,
Might in their working do you that offence,
Which else were shame, that then necessity
Will call discreet proceeding.

Fool
For, you trow, nuncle,

Hello there, daughter! What's that round your forehead?
I think you frown too much these days.

You were a good chap when you had no need to care about her frowning; now you are nothing:
I have more than you now; I am a fool, you are nothing.

Yes, all right, I will hold my tongue, that's what your face his ordering, although you say nothing.
Yum yum, the one who doesn't have crust or crumb,
when he's tired of everything will want some.

This one's an empty shell.

Not only, sir, your too much indulged fool,
but others from your insolent entourage
are always moaning and quarrelling; they break out
in unpleasant and intolerable riots. Sir,
I thought that by informing you about this
it was guaranteed something would be done; but now I wonder
considering what you also have said and done recently.
I hear that you defend this practice, and in fact encourage it; if this is true this mistake
will not go unpunished or unpaid for;
it might be thought that I would be
remiss in my duties as a daughter if I did this,
if it wasn't for the fact that everybody would recognise
that it had to be done.

Because, you know, nuncle,

The hedge-sparrow fed the cuckoo so long, That it's had it head bit off by it young. So, out went the candle, and we were left darkling.	the hedge sparrow fed the cuckoo for so long, that its head was bitten off by its young. So, out went the candle, and we were left in the dark.

KING LEAR
Are you our daughter?

Are you my daughter?

GONERIL
Come, sir,
I would you would make use of that good wisdom,
Whereof I know you are fraught; and put away
These dispositions, that of late transform you
From what you rightly are.

Come now, sir, I'd like you to use some of that good wisdom which I know you have plenty of; get rid of these states of mind, that have recently changed you from who you really are.

Fool
May not an ass know when the cart
draws the horse? Whoop, Jug! I love thee.

Even a fool can see when things are out of order. Hey there, jug! I love you.

KING LEAR
Doth any here know me? This is not Lear:
Doth Lear walk thus? speak thus? Where are his eyes?
Either his notion weakens, his discernings
Are lethargied--Ha! waking? 'tis not so.
Who is it that can tell me who I am?

Does anyone here know me? This can't be Lear: does Lear walk like this? Speak like this? Where are his eyes? Either his mind is weakened or his perception has darkened–ha! Am I awake? I can't be. Who can tell me who I am?

Fool
Lear's shadow.

You are Lear's shadow.

KING LEAR
I would learn that; for, by the
marks of sovereignty, knowledge, and reason,
I should be false persuaded I had daughters.

I want to know; because by the signs of sovereignty, knowledge, and wisdom, it doesn't look like I have any daughters.

Fool
Which they will make an obedient father.

And they will make their father obedient.

KING LEAR
Your name, fair gentlewoman?

What is your name, fair gentlewoman?

GONERIL
This admiration, sir, is much o' the savour
Of other your new pranks. I do beseech you

This pretence of wonder, sir, is much the same as your other new jokes. I must ask you

To understand my purposes aright:
As you are old and reverend, you should be wise.
Here do you keep a hundred knights and squires;
Men so disorder'd, so debosh'd and bold,
That this our court, infected with their manners,
Shows like a riotous inn: epicurism and lust
Make it more like a tavern or a brothel
Than a graced palace. The shame itself doth speak
For instant remedy: be then desired
By her, that else will take the thing she begs,
A little to disquantity your train;
And the remainder, that shall still depend,
To be such men as may besort your age,
And know themselves and you.

KING LEAR
Darkness and devils!
Saddle my horses; call my train together:
Degenerate bastard! I'll not trouble thee.
Yet have I left a daughter.

GONERIL
You strike my people; and your disorder'd rabble
Make servants of their betters.

Enter ALBANY

KING LEAR
Woe, that too late repents,--

To ALBANY
O, sir, are you come?
Is it your will? Speak, sir. Prepare my horses.
Ingratitude, thou marble-hearted fiend,
More hideous when thou show'st thee in a child
Than the sea-monster!

ALBANY
Pray, sir, be patient.

KING LEAR
[To GONERIL] Detested kite! thou liest.
My train are men of choice and rarest parts,

to understand what I mean:
as you are old and distinguished, you should be wise.
You keep a hundred knights and squires here;
they are men who are so disorderly, debauched and arrogant,
that our court, infected by their manners,
looks like a rowdy inn: greed and lust
make it more like a pub or brothel
than a gracious palace. This shame demands instant repair: so do as I ask,
or otherwise I will do it for you;
cut back on your retinue,
and the ones that you keep on
should be men suited to one of your age,
who have an idea of how to behave.

Darkness and devils!
Saddle my horses; gather my entourage:
degenerate bastard! I won't bother you.
I still have a daughter left.

You hit my people, and your disorderly rabble treat their betters like servants.

You will be sorry, too late–

Oh, you've come have you sir?
Is this what you want? Speak, sir. Get my horses ready.
Ingratitude, you hardhearted devil,
you are more revolting when you appear in a child than in a sea monster!

Please be patient, sir.

You foul kite! You are a liar.
My entourage are the best, most noble men,

41

That all particulars of duty know,
And in the most exact regard support
The worships of their name. O most small fault,
How ugly didst thou in Cordelia show!
That, like an engine, wrench'd my frame of nature
From the fix'd place; drew from heart all love,
And added to the gall. O Lear, Lear, Lear!
Beat at this gate, that let thy folly in,

Striking his head

And thy dear judgment out! Go, go, my people.

ALBANY
My lord, I am guiltless, as I am ignorant
Of what hath moved you.

KING LEAR
It may be so, my lord.
Hear, nature, hear; dear goddess, hear!
Suspend thy purpose, if thou didst intend
To make this creature fruitful!
Into her womb convey sterility!
Dry up in her the organs of increase;
And from her derogate body never spring
A babe to honour her! If she must teem,
Create her child of spleen; that it may live,
And be a thwart disnatured torment to her!
Let it stamp wrinkles in her brow of youth;
With cadent tears fret
Turn all her mother's pains and benefits
To laughter and contempt; that she may feel
How sharper than a serpent's tooth it is
To have a thankless child! Away, away!

Exit

ALBANY
Now, gods that we adore, whereof comes this?

GONERIL
Never afflict yourself to know the cause;
But let his disposition have that scope
That dotage gives it.

who know all there is to know about their duty, and know exactly how to maintain their honor. What a little fault it was that looked so ugly in Cordelia! It was like a machine that tore out my heart; it emptied my heart of love, and poured in bitterness. Oh Lear, Lear, Lear! Smash on this gate, that let your stupidity in

and let your common sense out! On you go, my people.

My lord, I am not guilty as I don't know what has upset you.

That may be the case, my lord. Listen, nature, listen! Dear goddess, listen! If you intended for this creature to bear children, suspend your plans! Make her womb sterile! Dry up her reproductive system; and never let her degenerate body produce a baby to honor her! If she must spawn, let her have a child made only of spleen: so it can live and be a twisted unloving torture to her! Let it stamp wrinkles onto her youthful brow; May storms of tears cut channels in her cheeks, greet all her motherly efforts and gifts with contempt and laughter, so she can feel how much sharper than a snake's tooth it is to have an ungrateful child! Come on, come on!

Now, by all the gods that we adore, what brought this on?

Don't bother trying to find out the reason; just let him carry on as senile old fools do.

Re-enter KING LEAR

KING LEAR
What, fifty of my followers at a clap!
Within a fortnight!

So, you want me to lose fifty of my followers in one go! Within a fortnight!

ALBANY
What's the matter, sir?

What's the matter, sir?

KING LEAR
I'll tell thee:

I'll tell you:

To GONERIL
Life and death! I am ashamed
That thou hast power to shake my manhood thus;
That these hot tears, which break from me perforce,
Should make thee worth them. Blasts and fogs upon thee!
The untented woundings of a father's curse
Pierce every sense about thee! Old fond eyes,
Beweep this cause again, I'll pluck ye out,
And cast you, with the waters that you lose,
To temper clay. Yea, it is come to this?
Let is be so: yet have I left a daughter,
Who, I am sure, is kind and comfortable:
When she shall hear this of thee, with her nails
She'll flay thy wolvish visage. Thou shalt find
That I'll resume the shape which thou dost think
I have cast off for ever: thou shalt,
I warrant thee.

By life and death! I'm ashamed that you can disturb me so much; if only you were worth these hot tears which I can't control. Curses and confusion to you!

Exeunt KING LEAR, KENT, and Attendants

GONERIL
Do you mark that, my lord?

Did you see that, my lord?

ALBANY
I cannot be so partial, Goneril,
To the great love I bear you,--

I cannot be so biased, Goneril, towards the great love I have for you–

GONERIL
Pray you, content. What, Oswald, ho!

Please, that's enough. Oswald, come here!

To the Fool

43

You, sir, more knave than fool, after your master.

Fool
Nuncle Lear, nuncle Lear, tarry and take the fool with thee.
A fox, when one has caught her,
And such a daughter,
Should sure to the slaughter,
If my cap would buy a halter:
So the fool follows after.

Exit

GONERIL
This man hath had good counsel:--a hundred knights!
'Tis politic and safe to let him keep
At point a hundred knights: yes, that, on every dream,
Each buzz, each fancy, each complaint, dislike,
He may enguard his dotage with their powers,
And hold our lives in mercy. Oswald, I say!

ALBANY
Well, you may fear too far.

GONERIL
Safer than trust too far:
Let me still take away the harms I fear,
Not fear still to be taken: I know his heart.
What he hath utter'd I have writ my sister
If she sustain him and his hundred knights
When I have show'd the unfitness,--

Re-enter OSWALD
How now, Oswald!
What, have you writ that letter to my sister?

OSWALD
Yes, madam.

GONERIL
Take you some company, and away to horse:
Inform her full of my particular fear;

You, sir, who is more of a knave than a fool, follow your master.

Nuncle Lear, nuncle Lear, wait and take the fool with you.
A trapped fox, when you've caught her,
and a daughter like this,
should be sent to the slaughter,
if my cap could pay for the rope:
and so the fool follows on.

This man has had good advice: a hundred knights!
Oh yes, it's a sensible and safe to let him keep a hundred armed knights: yes, so that with every dream,
every rumour, every imagining, every complaint or dislike
he can back up his senility with their power, and hold our lives in his hand. Oswald, here!

Well, you may be worrying too much.

That's better than not worrying enough: let me always remove the danger I fear rather than live in fear of danger: I know what he's like.
I have written to tell my sister what he said; if she supports him and his hundred knights after I have shown her why she shouldn't–

Hello there, Oswald!
Now, have you written that letter to my sister?

Yes, madam.

Take some men, and get on your horses: give her all the details about my personal fears;

And thereto add such reasons of your own
As may compact it more. Get you gone;
And hasten your return.

Exit OSWALD
No, no, my lord,
This milky gentleness and course of yours
Though I condemn not, yet, under pardon,
You are much more attask'd for want of wisdom
Than praised for harmful mildness.

ALBANY
How far your eyes may pierce I can not tell:
Striving to better, oft we mar what's well.

GONERIL
Nay, then--

ALBANY
Well, well; the event.

Exeunt

and add to it any reasons of your own which strengthen the case. Get going, and hurry back.

*No, no, my lord,
this soft gentleness and action of yours, although I don't condemn you for it, if you'll excuse me,
you're more to be criticised for a lack of wisdom than praised for a mildness which will do harm.*

I can't tell how well you've predicted the future: trying to improve things, we often damage the good things we have.

No, but–

All right, all right; we'll wait and see what happens.

SCENE V. Court before the same.

Enter KING LEAR, KENT, and Fool

KING LEAR
Go you before to Gloucester with these letters. Acquaint my daughter no further with any thing you know than comes from her demand out of the letter. If your diligence be not speedy, I shall be there afore you.

You go ahead with this letter to Gloucester. Don't tell my daughter about anything, except for answering any questions she has about the letter. If you don't hurry, I will be there before you.

KENT
I will not sleep, my lord, till I have delivered your letter.

I won't sleep, my lord, until I have delivered your letter.

Exit

Fool
If a man's brains were in's heels, were't not in danger of kibes?

If a man had brains in his heels, wouldn't he be in danger of chilblains?

KING LEAR
Ay, boy.

Yes, boy.

Fool
Then, I prithee, be merry; thy wit shall ne'er go slip-shod.

Then, I beg you, be happy; you haven't any brains to protect.

KING LEAR
Ha, ha, ha!

Hah, hah, hah!

Fool
Shalt see thy other daughter will use thee kindly; for though she's as like this as a crab's like an apple, yet I can tell what I can tell.

We shall see if your other daughter treats you well; although her and Goneril are two peas in a pod, I can see what I can see.

KING LEAR
Why, what canst thou tell, my boy?

What can you see, my boy?

Fool
She will taste as like this as a crab does to a crab. Thou canst tell why one's nose stands i' the middle on's face?

She will be just as bitter as this one. Do you know why your nose is in the middle of your face?

46

KING LEAR
No.

Fool
Why, to keep one's eyes of either side's nose; that
what a man cannot smell out, he may spy into.

KING LEAR
I did her wrong--

Fool
Canst tell how an oyster makes his shell?

KING LEAR
No.

Fool
Nor I neither; but I can tell why a snail has a house.

KING LEAR
Why?

Fool
Why, to put his head in; not to give it away to his
daughters, and leave his horns without a case.

KING LEAR
I will forget my nature. So kind a father! Be my horses ready?

Fool
Thy asses are gone about 'em. The reason why the
seven stars are no more than seven is a pretty reason.

KING LEAR
Because they are not eight?

Fool
Yes, indeed: thou wouldst make a good fool.

KING LEAR

No.

Why, to keep your eyes apart; so if you can't smell mischief, you can see it.

I did her wrong–

Do you know how an oyster makes his shell?

No.

Me neither; but I know why snail has a house.

Why?

Why, to keep his head in; not to give it away to his daughters, and leave himself unprotected.

I will go against my nature and stop being a kind father! Are my horses ready?

Your asses are seeing to them. There's a good reason why the seven stars are only seven.

Because there are not eight of them?

Yes indeed: you would make a good fool.

47

To take 't again perforce! Monster ingratitude! | *Perhaps I should take my kingdom back by force! The terrible ingratitude!*

Fool
If thou wert my fool, nuncle, I'ld have thee beaten
for being old before thy time.

*Nuncle, if you were my fool I would have you beaten
for being old before your time.*

KING LEAR
How's that?

What do you mean?

Fool
Thou shouldst not have been old till thou hadst been wise.

You should have got wise before you got old.

KING LEAR
O, let me not be mad, not mad, sweet heaven
Keep me in temper: I would not be mad!

Now don't let me go mad, not mad, dear heaven keep me calm: I don't want to go mad!

Enter Gentleman
How now! are the horses ready?

Hello there! Are the horses ready?

Gentleman
Ready, my lord.

They are ready my lord.

KING LEAR
Come, boy.

Come on, boy.

Fool
She that's a maid now, and laughs at my departure,
Shall not be a maid long, unless things be cut shorter.

*The one who's a virgin now, and laughs at my going,
won't be a virgin for long, unless we run out of time.*

Exeunt

Act 2

SCENE I. GLOUCESTER's castle.

Enter EDMUND, and CURAN meets him

EDMUND
Save thee, Curan.

God protect you, Curan.

CURAN
And you, sir. I have been with your father, and given him notice that the Duke of Cornwall and Regan
his duchess will be here with him this night.

And you, sir. I have been with your father, and told him that the Duke of Cornwall and Regan his Duchess will join him here tonight.

EDMUND
How comes that?

Why is this happening?

CURAN
Nay, I know not. You have heard of the news abroad;
I mean the whispered ones, for they are yet but ear-kissing arguments?

I can't say. You will have heard the news; I mean the whispered news, for what is it at the moment but gossip?

EDMUND
Not I pray you, what are they?

I've heard nothing, what is this news?

CURAN
Have you heard of no likely wars toward, 'twixt the
Dukes of Cornwall and Albany?

Haven't you heard that there is probably going to be a war between the Dukes of Cornwall and Albany?

EDMUND
Not a word.

I've not heard a word.

CURAN
You may do, then, in time. Fare you well, sir.

You may do, in time. Farewell, sir.

Exit

EDMUND
The duke be here to-night? The better! best!
This weaves itself perforce into my business.
My father hath set guard to take my brother;
And I have one thing, of a queasy question,
Which I must act: briefness and fortune, work!
Brother, a word; descend: brother, I say!

The Duke will be here tonight? That's better! That's the best! This plays nicely into my hands. My father has set guards to capture my brother; and I have some delicate business to attend to: speed and luck, work for me! Brother, let me have a word with you; come down: brother, I'm

50

Enter EDGAR
My father watches: O sir, fly this place;
Intelligence is given where you are hid;
You have now the good advantage of the night:
Have you not spoken 'gainst the Duke of
Cornwall?
He's coming hither: now, i' the night, i' the haste,
And Regan with him: have you nothing said
Upon his party 'gainst the Duke of Albany?
Advise yourself.

EDGAR
I am sure on't, not a word.

EDMUND
I hear my father coming: pardon me:
In cunning I must draw my sword upon you
Draw; seem to defend yourself; now quit you
well.
Yield: come before my father. Light, ho, here!
Fly, brother. Torches, torches! So, farewell.

Exit EDGAR
Some blood drawn on me would beget opinion.

Wounds his arm
Of my more fierce endeavour: I have seen
drunkards
Do more than this in sport. Father, father!
Stop, stop! No help?

Enter GLOUCESTER, and Servants with torches

GLOUCESTER
Now, Edmund, where's the villain?

EDMUND
Here stood he in the dark, his sharp sword out,
Mumbling of wicked charms, conjuring the
moon
To stand auspicious mistress,--

GLOUCESTER
But where is he?

calling!
My father is looking for you: sir, run away;
his spies know where you are hiding;
you now have darkness in your favour:
didn't you speak out against the Duke of
Cornwall?
He's coming here: now, tonight, and hurrying,
bringing Regan with him: have you ever said
anything in his favour, against the Duke of
Albany? Think carefully.

I am positive that I've said nothing.

I can hear my father coming: forgive me,
to look genuine I must draw my sword against
you; you draw yours, pretend to defend yourself,
now fight strongly. Surrender: come to my
father. Give me a light, here!
Run, brother. Bring the torches! So, farewell.

If I spill some blood people will think

I really fought well: I've seen
drunkards
do themselves more damage for fun. Father,
father! Stop, stop! Will nobody help me?

Now, Edmund, where is the villain?

He stood here in the dark, waving his sharp
sword, muttering about wicked spells, ordering
the moon
to come to his aid–

But where has he gone?

51

EDMUND
Look, sir, I bleed.

Looks sir, I am bleeding.

GLOUCESTER
Where is the villain, Edmund?

Edmund, where has the villain gone?

EDMUND
Fled this way, sir. When by no means he could--

He ran this way, sir. When there was no way for him–

GLOUCESTER
Pursue him, ho! Go after.

Chase him! Follow him.

Exeunt some Servants
By no means what?

No way for him to what?

EDMUND
Persuade me to the murder of your lordship;
But that I told him, the revenging gods
'Gainst parricides did all their thunders bend;
Spoke, with how manifold and strong a bond
The child was bound to the father; sir, in fine,
Seeing how loathly opposite I stood
To his unnatural purpose, in fell motion,
With his prepared sword, he charges home
My unprovided body, lanced mine arm:
But when he saw my best alarum'd spirits,
Bold in the quarrel's right, roused to the encounter,
Or whether gasted by the noise I made,
Full suddenly he fled.

Persuade me to help murder your lordship; instead I told him that the avenging gods throw down all their anger against those who kill the fathers; I told him how many strong bonds there are between a child and his father; to sum up, seeing how much I detested his unnatural plans he charged me with his already drawn sword against my un-armoured body, and pierced my arm: but when he saw that my blood was up, ready to fight, knowing I was in the right, or maybe he was frightened by the noise I made, he suddenly ran off.

GLOUCESTER
Let him fly far:
Not in this land shall he remain uncaught;
And found--dispatch. The noble duke my master,
My worthy arch and patron, comes to-night:
By his authority I will proclaim it,
That he which finds him shall deserve our thanks,
Bringing the murderous coward to the stake;
He that conceals him, death.

He can run as far as he likes; if he stays in this land he will be caught, and when he's caught he'll be killed. The noble Duke my master, my good patron and protector, is coming tonight: I shall use his authority to announce that whoever catches him will be rewarded for bringing the murderous coward to execution; and it will be death for anyone who hides him.

EDMUND
When I dissuaded him from his intent,

When I tried to dissuade him,

And found him pight to do it, with curst speech
I threaten'd to discover him: he replied,
'Thou unpossessing bastard! dost thou think,
If I would stand against thee, would the reposal
Of any trust, virtue, or worth in thee
Make thy words faith'd? No: what I should deny,--
As this I would: ay, though thou didst produce
My very character,--I'ld turn it all
To thy suggestion, plot, and damned practise:
And thou must make a dullard of the world,
If they not thought the profits of my death
Were very pregnant and potential spurs
To make thee seek it.'

*and found he was determined to do it, I cursed him
and threatened to unmask him: he answered,
'You landless bastard! Do you think,
with me on the other side, that anybody would
give any trust, virtue or value to any words
you might swear? No: if I denied it–
as I would, even if you could produce
irrefutable evidence–I would blame it all
on your idea, plot and evil execution:
and the whole world would be very stupid
if they didn't see that you were the one
who was motivated by the profits
which my death would bring you.'*

GLOUCESTER
Strange and fasten'd villain
Would he deny his letter? I never got him.

*Unnatural and hardened scoundrel,
would he deny he wrote that letter? He's no child of mine.*

Tucket within
Hark, the duke's trumpets! I know not why he comes.
All ports I'll bar; the villain shall not 'scape;
The duke must grant me that: besides, his picture
I will send far and near, that all the kingdom
May have the due note of him; and of my land,
Loyal and natural boy, I'll work the means
To make thee capable.

*Listen, it's the Duke's trumpets! I don't know why he's here.
I shall block all the ports; the villain will not escape;
the Duke must promise me that: also, I will send his picture far and wide, so that the whole kingdom will know what he looks like; and as for my land my loyal and natural son, I'll make sure that you can inherit it.*

Enter CORNWALL, REGAN, and Attendants

CORNWALL
How now, my noble friend! since I came hither,
Which I can call but now, I have heard strange news.

Hello, my noble friend! Since I arrived, just a moment ago, I have heard strange news.

REGAN
If it be true, all vengeance comes too short
Which can pursue the offender. How dost, my lord?

If it's true, you can't get hold of the offender quickly enough. How are you, my lord?

GLOUCESTER
O, madam, my old heart is crack'd, it's crack'd!

O madam, my old heart is broken, it's broken!

REGAN

53

What, did my father's godson seek your life?
He whom my father named? your Edgar?

GLOUCESTER
O, lady, lady, shame would have it hid!

REGAN
Was he not companion with the riotous knights
That tend upon my father?

GLOUCESTER
I know not, madam: 'tis too bad, too bad.

EDMUND
Yes, madam, he was of that consort.

REGAN
No marvel, then, though he were ill affected:
'Tis they have put him on the old man's death,
To have the expense and waste of his revenues.
I have this present evening from my sister
Been well inform'd of them; and with such cautions,
That if they come to sojourn at my house,
I'll not be there.

CORNWALL
Nor I, assure thee, Regan.
Edmund, I hear that you have shown your father
A child-like office.

EDMUND
'Twas my duty, sir.

GLOUCESTER
He did bewray his practise; and received
This hurt you see, striving to apprehend him.

CORNWALL
Is he pursued?

GLOUCESTER
Ay, my good lord.

CORNWALL

---

*What, did my father's godson try to kill you?
The one my father named? Your Edgar?*

O lady, lady, I wish for shame that it was hidden.

Didn't he hang around with the rowdy knights who served my father?

I don't know, madam: it's awful, awful.

Yes madam, he was one of that band.

*It's no wonder then that he has turned bad: they will have encouraged him to kill the old man,
so that they can get their hands on his money.
My sister has, this very evening,
told me all about them; because of her warning if they come to stay at my house
I won't be there.*

*Me neither, I promise, Regan.
Edmund, I hear that you have done your best for your father.*

It was my duty sir.

He discovered what he was up to, and got this wound that you can see, trying to catch him.

Is he being pursued?

Yes, my good lord.

If he be taken, he shall never more
Be fear'd of doing harm: make your own purpose,
How in my strength you please. For you, Edmund,
Whose virtue and obedience doth this instant
So much commend itself, you shall be ours:
Natures of such deep trust we shall much need;
You we first seize on.

EDMUND
I shall serve you, sir,
Truly, however else.

GLOUCESTER
For him I thank your grace.

CORNWALL
You know not why we came to visit you,--

REGAN
Thus out of season, threading dark-eyed night:
Occasions, noble Gloucester, of some poise,
Wherein we must have use of your advice:
Our father he hath writ, so hath our sister,
Of differences, which I least thought it fit
To answer from our home; the several messengers
From hence attend dispatch. Our good old friend,
Lay comforts to your bosom; and bestow
Your needful counsel to our business,
Which craves the instant use.

GLOUCESTER
I serve you, madam:
Your graces are right welcome.

Exeunt

If he is caught, no one will ever have to be afraid of him again: make your plans, use my resources as you like. As for you, Edmund, whose virtue and obedience at this time is so commendable, you shall serve us: we have great need of such trustworthy people; we choose you first.

I shall serve you, sir, loyally, whatever happens.

I thank your Grace on his behalf.

You don't know why we came to visit you—

At the wrong time of year, sneaking through the night: there are things happening, noble Gloucester, of some importance, which you must advise us about: our father has written, so has our sister, that they have fallen out, and I thought it best not to deal with them at home; I have several messengers waiting to be sent out. Our good old friend, be of good heart, and give your needed advice to these matters, which must be addressed at once.

I am at your service, madam: both of you are very welcome.

SCENE II. Before Gloucester's castle.

Enter KENT and OSWALD, severally

OSWALD
Good dawning to thee, friend: art of this house?

Good morning to you, friend: are you part of this household?

KENT
Ay.

Yes.

OSWALD
Where may we set our horses?

Where should we put our horses?

KENT
I' the mire.

In the swamp.

OSWALD
Prithee, if thou lovest me, tell me.

Please, if you like me, tell me.

KENT
I love thee not.

I don't like you.

OSWALD
Why, then, I care not for thee.

Well then, I don't like you.

KENT
If I had thee in Lipsbury pinfold, I would make thee
care for me.

If I had you under my power, I would make you like me.

OSWALD
Why dost thou use me thus? I know thee not.

Why are you treating me like this? I don't know you.

KENT
Fellow, I know thee.

My man, I know you.

OSWALD
What dost thou know me for?

What do you know of me?

KENT
A knave; a rascal; an eater of broken meats; a
base, proud, shallow, beggarly, three-suited,
hundred-pound, filthy, worsted-stocking knave; a
lily-livered, action-taking knave, a whoreson,

*I know that you're a knave, a rascal, a scrounger,
low, arrogant, shallow, begging, serving,
bribing, filthy, lowborn knave; a
lily-livered, lawsuit starting knave, son of a*

56

glass-gazing, super-serviceable finical rogue; one-trunk-inheriting slave; one that wouldst be a bawd, in way of good service, and art nothing but
the composition of a knave, beggar, coward, pandar,
and the son and heir of a mongrel bitch: one whom I
will beat into clamorous whining, if thou deniest the least syllable of thy addition.

OSWALD
Why, what a monstrous fellow art thou, thus to rail
on one that is neither known of thee nor knows thee!

KENT
What a brazen-faced varlet art thou, to deny thou
knowest me! Is it two days ago since I tripped up
thy heels, and beat thee before the king? Draw, you
rogue: for, though it be night, yet the moon shines; I'll make a sop o' the moonshine of you: draw, you whoreson cullionly barber-monger, draw.

Drawing his sword

OSWALD
Away! I have nothing to do with thee.

KENT
Draw, you rascal: you come with letters against the
king; and take vanity the puppet's part against the
royalty of her father: draw, you rogue, or I'll so carbonado your shanks: draw, you rascal; come your ways.

OSWALD
Help, ho! murder! help!

---

whore,
vain, officious, affected rogue;
a poor slave; one who would be a pimp, to do himself good, and you are nothing but a combination of knave, beggar, coward, pimp, and the son and heir of a mongrel bitch: one whom I
will beat until he begs me to stop, if you deny anything on this list.

Why, what a terrible man you are, to launch such an attack
on someone you don't know and who doesn't know you!

What a cheeky scoundrel you are, to deny that you
know me! Wasn't it just two days ago that I tripped you up
and beat you in front of the King? Draw, you rogue; although it's night, the moon is out; I'll let the moonshine into you:
draw, you vile vain son of a whore, draw.

Get lost! I've got no quarrel with you.

Draw, you rascal: you are carrying letters against the
King, and you have taken the side of that vain puppet against the royalty of her father: draw, you rogue, or I'll
make mincemeat of you: draw, you rascal, bring it on.

Bring me help! Murder! Help!

KENT
Strike, you slave; stand, rogue, stand; you neat slave, strike.

Fight, you slave; stand up, you rogue; you foppish slave, fight.

Beating him

OSWALD
Help, ho! murder! murder!

Help, here! Murder! Murder!

Enter EDMUND, with his rapier drawn, CORNWALL, REGAN, GLOUCESTER, and Servants

EDMUND
How now! What's the matter?

What's this! What's the quarrel?

KENT
With you, goodman boy, an you please: come, I'll
flesh ye; come on, young master.

*It's with you, you cheeky boy, if you want it to be: come on, I'll
teach you; come on, little man.*

GLOUCESTER
Weapons! arms! What 's the matter here?

Weapons! Fighting! What's the argument about?

CORNWALL
Keep peace, upon your lives:
He dies that strikes again. What is the matter?

Stop this, if you value your lives: whoever carries on is dead. Why are you fighting?

REGAN
The messengers from our sister and the king.

These are the messengers from my sister and the King.

CORNWALL
What is your difference? speak.

What are you quarrelling about? Speak.

OSWALD
I am scarce in breath, my lord.

I can hardly breathe, my lord.

KENT
No marvel, you have so bestirred your valour. You
cowardly rascal, nature disclaims in thee: a tailor made thee.

*It's no wonder, you've put such a strain on your bravery.
You cowardly rascal, you can't be a real man: you're made of cloth.*

CORNWALL
Thou art a strange fellow: a tailor make a man?

You are a strange fellow: a man made by a tailor?

58

KENT
Ay, a tailor, sir: a stone-cutter or painter could not have made him so ill, though he had been but two
hours at the trade.

CORNWALL
Speak yet, how grew your quarrel?

OSWALD
This ancient ruffian, sir, whose life I have spared
at suit of his gray beard,--

KENT
Thou whoreson zed! thou unnecessary letter! My
lord, if you will give me leave, I will tread this unbolted villain into mortar, and daub the wall of
a jakes with him. Spare my gray beard, you wagtail?

CORNWALL
Peace, sirrah!
You beastly knave, know you no reverence?

KENT
Yes, sir; but anger hath a privilege.

CORNWALL
Why art thou angry?

KENT
That such a slave as this should wear a sword,
Who wears no honesty. Such smiling rogues as these,
Like rats, oft bite the holy cords a-twain
Which are too intrinse t' unloose; smooth every passion
That in the natures of their lords rebel;
Bring oil to fire, snow to their colder moods;
Renege, affirm, and turn their halcyon beaks
With every gale and vary of their masters,
Knowing nought, like dogs, but following.
A plague upon your epileptic visage!

*Yes, a tailor, sir: a mason or a painter would not
have made such a bad job of it, even if he had only been in business for a couple of hours.*

Now speak, what started your argument?

This old scoundrel, sir, whose life I have spared out of respect for his grey beard–

*You worthless Z! You unnecessary letter! My lord, if you allow me, I will crush this effeminate rascal into plaster, and cover the walls
of a toilet with him. Spare my grey beard, you bantamweight?*

*Be quiet, sir!
You beastly knave, have you no respect?*

Yes, sir, but anger is allowed to take liberties.

Why are you angry?

*To see that a slave like this has a sword, when he has no honesty. Smiling rascals like this,
like rats, often bite the sacred bonds apart which are too strongly knotted to untie; they encourage
every passion that blows up in their lord's minds; they throw oil on the fire, add snow when they are cold; they betray, swear, and spin around like weathervanes at every gale and gust from their masters; like dogs, they only know how to follow. A curse upon your twitching face!*

Smile you my speeches, as I were a fool?
Goose, if I had you upon Sarum plain,
I'd drive ye cackling home to Camelot.

CORNWALL
Why, art thou mad, old fellow?

GLOUCESTER
How fell you out? say that.

KENT
No contraries hold more antipathy
Than I and such a knave.

CORNWALL
Why dost thou call him a knave? What's his offence?

KENT
His countenance likes me not.

CORNWALL
No more, perchance, does mine, nor his, nor hers.

KENT
Sir, 'tis my occupation to be plain:
I have seen better faces in my time
Than stands on any shoulder that I see
Before me at this instant.

CORNWALL
This is some fellow,
Who, having been praised for bluntness, doth affect
A saucy roughness, and constrains the garb
Quite from his nature: he cannot flatter, he,
An honest mind and plain, he must speak truth!
An they will take it, so; if not, he's plain.
These kind of knaves I know, which in this plainness
Harbour more craft and more corrupter ends
Than twenty silly ducking observants
That stretch their duties nicely.

Do you smile at my speech, as if I were a fool?
You goose, if I had you on Salisbury plain,
I'd drive you cackling home to Winchester.

What, old fellow, are you mad?

Tell us what caused the argument.

There are no two such opposites
as me and a scoundrel like this.

Why are you calling him a scoundrel? What's he done?

I don't like his face.

And maybe you don't like mine, or his, or hers.

Sir, it's my job to be straightforward:
I have seen better faces in my time
than any of the ones
I can see at the moment.

This is some chap who,
having been praised for plain speaking, now
tries a coarse cheekiness, and twists his speech
into double meanings: he likes to think he will
not flatter, that he has an honest plain mind, so
he must speak the truth!
People have to believe him, if they don't he's
uncovered. I know these kind of scoundrels, in
their blunt speaking
they have more trickery and corrupt plans
than twenty backside kissing servants
doing their duties as well as they can.

KENT
Sir, in good sooth, in sincere verity,
Under the allowance of your great aspect,
Whose influence, like the wreath of radiant fire
On flickering Phoebus' front,--

Sir, in good faith, with sincere truth, with the permission of your noble face, whose influence, like the ring of radiant fire flickering around the sun–

CORNWALL
What mean'st by this?

What do you mean by this?

KENT
To go out of my dialect, which you discommend so much. I know, sir, I am no flatterer: he that beguiled you in a plain accent was a plain knave; which for my part I will not be, though I should win your displeasure
to entreat me to 't.

I'm changing my speech, which you so disapproved of. I know, sir, that I am no flatterer: when you have been tripped in a plain accent you have been tricked by a plain knave; I will not be such a person, even if you don't like it.

CORNWALL
What was the offence you gave him?

How did you offend him?

OSWALD
I never gave him any:
It pleased the king his master very late
To strike at me, upon his misconstruction;
When he, conjunct and flattering his displeasure,
Tripp'd me behind; being down, insulted, rail'd,
And put upon him such a deal of man,
That worthied him, got praises of the king
For him attempting who was self-subdued;
And, in the fleshment of this dread exploit,
Drew on me here again.

I didn't: recently his master the King decided to hit me, due to being misled by him; when he, joining in and backing up his anger, tripped me from behind; once I was down he insulted and ranted at me, made out he was such a great man to get himself honour, and got praise from the King for attacking someone who was controlling himself; and in his excitement at this foul deed he decided to try it on with me again here.

KENT
None of these rogues and cowards
But Ajax is their fool.

There's not one of these rogues and cowards who doesn't think he's a great warrior.

CORNWALL
Fetch forth the stocks!
You stubborn ancient knave, you reverend braggart,
We'll teach you--

Bring out the stocks! You stubborn old knave, you old braggart, we'll teach you–

KENT
Sir, I am too old to learn:
Call not your stocks for me: I serve the king;

Sir, I am too old to learn: don't bring out your stocks for me: I serve the

61

On whose employment I was sent to you:
You shall do small respect, show too bold malice
Against the grace and person of my master,
Stocking his messenger.

CORNWALL
Fetch forth the stocks! As I have life and honour,
There shall he sit till noon.

REGAN
Till noon! till night, my lord; and all night too.

KENT
Why, madam, if I were your father's dog,
You should not use me so.

REGAN
Sir, being his knave, I will.

CORNWALL
This is a fellow of the self-same colour
Our sister speaks of. Come, bring away the stocks!

Stocks brought out

GLOUCESTER
Let me beseech your grace not to do so:
His fault is much, and the good king his master
Will cheque him for 't: your purposed low correction
Is such as basest and contemned'st wretches
For pilferings and most common trespasses
Are punish'd with: the king must take it ill,
That he's so slightly valued in his messenger,
Should have him thus restrain'd.

CORNWALL
I'll answer that.

REGAN
My sister may receive it much more worse,
To have her gentleman abused, assaulted,

King; I was sent to you on his orders:
you won't be showing any respect, you'll be attacking
the dignity and the person of my master
if you put me in the stocks.

Bring out the stocks! I swear on my life and honor
that he will sit there until noon.

Till noon! Till night, my lord; and all night too.

Why, madam, you shouldn't treat me like this
if I was your father's dog.

Sir, as you are his knave, I will.

This looks like one of those fellows our sister
warned us about. Come on, bring the stocks!

Let me beg your Grace not to do this:
he is most in the wrong, and the good King, his
master, will make him pay for it: your intended punishment
is given to the lowest most hated wretches
for petty theft and other minor offences:
the King will certainly take offence
to see that his messenger gets so little respect
that he is locked up like this.

I'll risk that.

My sister would take it far worse
to see her gentleman had been abused and

62

For following her affairs. Put in his legs.

KENT is put in the stocks
Come, my good lord, away.

Exeunt all but GLOUCESTER and KENT

GLOUCESTER
I am sorry for thee, friend; 'tis the duke's pleasure,
Whose disposition, all the world well knows,
Will not be rubb'd nor stopp'd: I'll entreat for thee.

KENT
Pray, do not, sir: I have watched and travell'd hard;
Some time I shall sleep out, the rest I'll whistle.
A good man's fortune may grow out at heels:
Give you good morrow!

GLOUCESTER
The duke's to blame in this; 'twill be ill taken.

Exit

KENT
Good king, that must approve the common saw,
Thou out of heaven's benediction comest
To the warm sun!
Approach, thou beacon to this under globe,
That by thy comfortable beams I may
Peruse this letter! Nothing almost sees miracles
But misery: I know 'tis from Cordelia,
Who hath most fortunately been inform'd
Of my obscured course; and shall find time
From this enormous state, seeking to give
Losses their remedies. All weary and o'erwatch'd,
Take vantage, heavy eyes, not to behold
This shameful lodging.
Fortune, good night: smile once more: turn thy wheel!

Sleeps

assaulted when going about her business. Put in his legs.

Come on, my good lord, let's go

*I am sorry for you my friend; this is the Duke's whim,
and all the world knows that once his mind is made up he can't be stopped or changed: I'll put in a word for you.*

*Please don't, Sir: I have gone without sleep and have a hard journey;
I will get some sleep and the rest of the time whistle. A good man can be down on his luck: good day to you!*

The Duke's to blame for this; this will not be well received.

*Good King, you are proving the old proverb jumping out of the frying pan
into the fire!
Come on, you lamp of the Earth,
so that I can use your handy sunbeams to read this letter! When we are miserable we love any relief: I know it's from Cordelia, who very luckily has been told
about my secret plans; she will find the time in this lawless state of affairs to make good these losses. I'm tired, I've been up too long, let my heavy eyelids fall so that I can't see the shameful place I'm in.
Good night, Fortune: shine on me once again: spin the wheel!*

SCENE III. A wood.

Enter EDGAR

EDGAR
I heard myself proclaim'd;
And by the happy hollow of a tree
Escaped the hunt. No port is free; no place,
That guard, and most unusual vigilance,
Does not attend my taking. Whiles I may 'scape,
I will preserve myself: and am bethought
To take the basest and most poorest shape
That ever penury, in contempt of man,
Brought near to beast: my face I'll grime with filth;
Blanket my loins: elf all my hair in knots;
And with presented nakedness out-face
The winds and persecutions of the sky.
The country gives me proof and precedent
Of Bedlam beggars, who, with roaring voices,
Strike in their numb'd and mortified bare arms
Pins, wooden pricks, nails, sprigs of rosemary;
And with this horrible object, from low farms,
Poor pelting villages, sheep-cotes, and mills,
Sometime with lunatic bans, sometime with prayers,
Enforce their charity. Poor Turlygod! poor Tom!
That's something yet: Edgar I nothing am.

I heard them calling my name and luckily found a hollow tree to hide from my pursuers. There is no port I can escape from and no place that's not heavily guarded, looking out to capture me. While I can stay free I will look after myself; I plan to take on the lowest and poorest appearance that poverty ever inflicted on a man, bringing him to the level of an animal; I'll smear my face with filth, wear a blanket around my waist, tangle my hair into knots, and naked I will confront the winds and rain. Around the country I have seen examples of mad beggars, who, with roaring voices, stick pins, spikes, nails, sprigs of rosemary, into their numbed and senseless bare arms; this horrible sight, in low farms, tiny poor villages, sheep pens, and mills, sometimes draws mad curses, sometimes prayers. Poor Turlygod! Poor Tom! I can be something as a beggar: I am no longer Edgar.

Exit

SCENE IV. Before GLOUCESTER's castle. KENT in the stocks.

Enter KING LEAR, Fool, and Gentleman

KING LEAR
'Tis strange that they should so depart from home,
And not send back my messenger.

It's strange that they should leave their home, and not answer my message.

Gentleman
As I learn'd,
The night before there was no purpose in them
Of this remove.

As far as I know the night before they had no intention of making this move.

KENT
Hail to thee, noble master!

Greetings, noble master!

KING LEAR
Ha!
Makest thou this shame thy pastime?

Ha! Are you having a game with this shame?

KENT
No, my lord.

No, my lord.

Fool
Ha, ha! he wears cruel garters. Horses are tied by the heads, dogs and bears by the neck, monkeys by
the loins, and men by the legs: when a man's over-lusty at legs, then he wears wooden nether-stocks.

Ha ha! He's wearing cruel garters. Horses are tied by the head, dogs and bears by the neck, monkeys round the waist, and men by the legs: when a man is inclined to jump about they put wooden stockings on him.

KING LEAR
What's he that hath so much thy place mistook
To set thee here?

Who is he who's shown your position so little respect that he's put you here?

KENT
It is both he and she;
Your son and daughter.

Both a he and a she; your son and your daughter.

KING LEAR
No.

No.

KENT
Yes.

Yes.

65

KING LEAR
No, I say.

KENT
I say, yea.

KING LEAR
No, no, they would not.

KENT
Yes, they have.

KING LEAR
By Jupiter, I swear, no.

KENT
By Juno, I swear, ay.

KING LEAR
They durst not do 't;
They could not, would not do 't; 'tis worse than murder,
To do upon respect such violent outrage:
Resolve me, with all modest haste, which way
Thou mightst deserve, or they impose, this usage,
Coming from us.

KENT
My lord, when at their home
I did commend your highness' letters to them,
Ere I was risen from the place that show'd
My duty kneeling, came there a reeking post,
Stew'd in his haste, half breathless, panting forth
From Goneril his mistress salutations;
Deliver'd letters, spite of intermission,
Which presently they read: on whose contents,
They summon'd up their meiny, straight took horse;
Commanded me to follow, and attend
The leisure of their answer; gave me cold looks:
And meeting here the other messenger,
Whose welcome, I perceived, had poison'd mine,--
Being the very fellow that of late

No, I say.

And I say yes.

No, no, they wouldn't.

Yes, they have.

By Jupiter I swear they would not.

By Juno I swear that they have.

*They wouldn't dare;
they could not, would not do it; it's worse than murder,
to commit such a disrespectful act:
tell me, as quickly as you can, how
you came to deserve, or them to impose, this punishment,
when you came from me.*

*My lord, when I went to their home
I gave them your Highness' letters;
before I had got up from where I was kneeling
to show my respect, there came a stinking
messenger, boiling with haste, almost out of
breath, gasping out greetings from his mistress,
Goneril; he delivered letters, in spite of the fact
that it interrupted me, which they then read:
having read them
they called up their servants, and got their horses ready;
they ordered me to follow and wait
for their answer; they gave me dirty looks:
and they met the other messenger here,
who I saw had managed to poison my welcome,
being the same fellow who recently*

66

Display'd so saucily against your highness,-- / was so cheeky to your Highness having more
Having more man than wit about me, drew: / courage than sense I drew my sword, and he
He raised the house with loud and coward cries. / woke the household with loud cowardly cries.
Your son and daughter found this trespass worth / Your son and daughter decided this offence
The shame which here it suffers. / deserved the punishment you can see here.

Fool
Winter's not gone yet, if the wild-geese fly that way. / Winter hasn't gone, if we see such migration.
Fathers that wear rags / Fathers that are poor
Do make their children blind; / are ignored by their children;
But fathers that bear bags / but fathers that are rich
Shall see their children kind. / will be well treated by them.
Fortune, that arrant whore, / Fortune, that flighty whore,
Ne'er turns the key to the poor. / never opens the door to the poor.
But, for all this, thou shalt have as many dolours / But despite this you shall have as many dollars
for thy daughters as thou canst tell in a year. / from your daughters as you could count in a year.

KING LEAR
O, how this mother swells up toward my heart! / Oh, how this choking feeling clutches at my
Hysterica passio, down, thou climbing sorrow, / heart! Get down you hysterical passion, you
Thy element's below! Where is this daughter? / rising depression, you should stay down below! Where is my daughter?

KENT
With the earl, sir, here within. / With the earl, sir, in there.

KING LEAR
Follow me not; / Don't follow me;
Stay here. / stay here.

Exit

Gentleman
Made you no more offence but what you speak of? / Did you do no other wrong except what you mentioned?

KENT
None. / Nothing.
How chance the king comes with so small a train? / Why has the King come with such a small entourage?

Fool
And thou hadst been set i' the stocks for that / If you were in the stocks for asking
question, thou hadst well deserved it. / that question, you would deserve it.

KENT

67

Why, fool?

Fool
We'll set thee to school to an ant, to teach thee
there's no labouring i' the winter. All that follow
their noses are led by their eyes but blind men;
and
there's not a nose among twenty but can smell
him
that's stinking. Let go thy hold when a great
wheel
runs down a hill, lest it break thy neck with
following it: but the great one that goes up the
hill, let him draw thee after. When a wise man
gives thee better counsel, give me mine again: I
would have none but knaves follow it, since a
fool gives it.
That sir which serves and seeks for gain,
And follows but for form,
Will pack when it begins to rain,
And leave thee in the storm,
But I will tarry; the fool will stay,
And let the wise man fly:
The knave turns fool that runs away;
The fool no knave, perdy.

KENT
Where learned you this, fool?

Fool
Not i' the stocks, fool.

Re-enter KING LEAR with GLOUCESTER

KING LEAR
Deny to speak with me? They are sick? they are
weary?
They have travell'd all the night? Mere fetches;
The images of revolt and flying off.
Fetch me a better answer.

GLOUCESTER
My dear lord,
You know the fiery quality of the duke;
How unremoveable and fix'd he is

Why, fool?

*We should get you an ant as your teacher, to show you
that nothing can be gained in the winter.
Everyone can sense the King's in trouble.
When a great wheel runs out of control downhill
let go of it, in case you break your neck in the chase;
but when a great one is going upwards
let him pull you behind him;
if you get better advice from a wise man
then give me mine back: only knaves
should follow it, because it's given by a fool.
The ones who serve and look for profit,
and only follow rank,
will pack up when it begins to rain
and leave you in the storm.
But I will wait; the fool will stay,
and let the wise man run:
the knave who runs away is a fool;
and this fool is no treacherous knave.*

Where did you learn this, fool?

Not in the stocks, fool.

*They won't speak with me? They are sick? They are tired?
They have been travelling all night? These are
just excuses; they show rebellion and evasion.
Get me a better answer.*

*My dear lord,
you know how fiery the Duke is;
you know how impossible it is*

68

In his own course.

KING LEAR
Vengeance! plague! death! confusion!
Fiery? what quality? Why, Gloucester, Gloucester,
I'ld speak with the Duke of Cornwall and his wife.

GLOUCESTER
Well, my good lord, I have inform'd them so.

KING LEAR
Inform'd them! Dost thou understand me, man?

GLOUCESTER
Ay, my good lord.

KING LEAR
The king would speak with Cornwall; the dear father
Would with his daughter speak, commands her service:
Are they inform'd of this? My breath and blood!
Fiery? the fiery duke? Tell the hot duke that--
No, but not yet: may be he is not well:
Infirmity doth still neglect all office
Whereto our health is bound; we are not ourselves
When nature, being oppress'd, commands the mind
To suffer with the body: I'll forbear;
And am fall'n out with my more headier will,
To take the indisposed and sickly fit
For the sound man. Death on my state! wherefore

Looking on KENT
Should he sit here? This act persuades me
That this remotion of the duke and her
Is practise only. Give me my servant forth.
Go tell the duke and 's wife I'ld speak with them,
Now, presently: bid them come forth and hear me,
Or at their chamber-door I'll beat the drum
Till it cry sleep to death.

to get him to deviate from his plans.

*Revenge! Plague! Death! Confusion!
Fiery? What's that? Why, Gloucester, Gloucester,
I will speak with the Duke of Cornwall and his wife.*

Well my good lord, that's what I have told them.

Told them! Do you understand what I've said, man?

Yes, my good lord.

*The King wants to speak with Cornwall; the dear father
wants to speak with his daughter, and orders her to obey:
have they been told this? By my breath and blood!
Fiery? The fiery Duke? Tell the hot Duke that—
no, not yet: maybe he really is not well:
when we are ill we forget all the duties
for which we need our health; we are not ourselves
when nature, under pressure, orders the mind
to suffer with the body: I'll hold back;
and I will control my temper
rather than think that the ill man
is representative of the healthy one.*

*Should he be sitting here? This act makes me
think that the aloofness of the Duke and her
is just a cover. Bring my servant here.
Go until the Duke and his wife that I want to speak to them, Right now: tell them to come out and listen to me,
or I will play the drums on their bedroom door until all sleep is impossible.*

69

GLOUCESTER
I would have all well betwixt you.

I would like everything to be well between you.

Exit

KING LEAR
O me, my heart, my rising heart! but, down!

Oh Lord, my heart, my swelling heart! Calm down!

Fool
Cry to it, nuncle, as the cockney did to the eels
when she put 'em i' the paste alive; she knapped 'em
o' the coxcombs with a stick, and cried 'Down,
wantons, down!' 'Twas her brother that, in pure
kindness to his horse, buttered his hay.

Shout at it, nuncle, like the Cockney did to the eels when she put them in the pie still alive; she bashed them over the head with a stick, shouting "down, you playful creatures, down!" However it was her brother who, just to be kind to his horse, put grease on his hay.

Enter CORNWALL, REGAN, GLOUCESTER, and Servants

KING LEAR
Good morrow to you both.

Good day to you both.

CORNWALL
Hail to your grace!

Greetings to your Grace!

KENT is set at liberty

REGAN
I am glad to see your highness.

I'm glad to see your Highness.

KING LEAR
Regan, I think you are; I know what reason
I have to think so: if thou shouldst not be glad,
I would divorce me from thy mother's tomb,
Sepulchring an adultress.

Regan, I believe you are; I'll tell you why I think so: if you weren't glad, I would divorce your dead mother as it would mean she was an adulteress.

To KENT
O, are you free?
Some other time for that. Beloved Regan,
Thy sister's naught: O Regan, she hath tied
Sharp-tooth'd unkindness, like a vulture, here:

Oh, are you free? We'll deal with that some other time. Beloved Regan, your sister is nothing: oh Regan, she has stabbed me with her unkindness, like a vulture, here:

Points to his heart
I can scarce speak to thee; thou'lt not believe
With how depraved a quality--O Regan!

I can hardly bring myself to talk about it; you will not believe how evil she has proved–oh Regan!

70

REGAN
I pray you, sir, take patience: I have hope.
You less know how to value her desert
Than she to scant her duty.

KING LEAR
Say, how is that?

REGAN
I cannot think my sister in the least
Would fail her obligation: if, sir, perchance
She have restrain'd the riots of your followers,
'Tis on such ground, and to such wholesome end,
As clears her from all blame.

KING LEAR
My curses on her!

REGAN
O, sir, you are old.
Nature in you stands on the very verge
Of her confine: you should be ruled and led
By some discretion, that discerns your state
Better than you yourself. Therefore, I pray you,
That to our sister you do make return;
Say you have wrong'd her, sir.

KING LEAR
Ask her forgiveness?
Do you but mark how this becomes the house:
'Dear daughter, I confess that I am old;

Kneeling
Age is unnecessary: on my knees I beg
That you'll vouchsafe me raiment, bed, and food.'

REGAN
Good sir, no more; these are unsightly tricks:
Return you to my sister.

KING LEAR
[Rising] Never, Regan:
She hath abated me of half my train;

*Please sir, be patient: I have hopes.
It's surely more likely that you have misunderstood her
than that she is neglecting her duty.*

What are you talking about?

*I can't imagine that my sister would ever
fail to do her duty: maybe, sir, if
she has stopped your followers' rowdiness
it was for good reasons and for a good end,
which would absolve her of all blame.*

My curses on her!

*Oh, sir, you are old.
Life has almost run its course
in you: you should be ruled and guided
by the wisdom of others, who can see your
position more clearly than you. So, I ask you,
to make it up to my sister;
admit that you have wronged her, sir.*

*Ask her forgiveness?
Think how this would befit my dignity:
'Dear daughter, I confess that I am old;*

*old people are useless: I'm begging you on my knees
to please let me have clothes, food and a bed.'*

*Stop this, good sir; these are silly tricks:
go back to my sister.*

*Never, Regan:
she took away half my entourage;*

71

Look'd black upon me; struck me with her tongue,
Most serpent-like, upon the very heart:
All the stored vengeances of heaven fall
On her ingrateful top! Strike her young bones,
You taking airs, with lameness!

CORNWALL
Fie, sir, fie!

KING LEAR
You nimble lightnings, dart your blinding flames
Into her scornful eyes! Infect her beauty,
You fen-suck'd fogs, drawn by the powerful sun,
To fall and blast her pride!

REGAN
O the blest gods! so will you wish on me,
When the rash mood is on.

KING LEAR
No, Regan, thou shalt never have my curse:
Thy tender-hefted nature shall not give
Thee o'er to harshness: her eyes are fierce; but thine
Do comfort and not burn. 'Tis not in thee
To grudge my pleasures, to cut off my train,
To bandy hasty words, to scant my sizes,
And in conclusion to oppose the bolt
Against my coming in: thou better know'st
The offices of nature, bond of childhood,
Effects of courtesy, dues of gratitude;
Thy half o' the kingdom hast thou not forgot,
Wherein I thee endow'd.

REGAN
Good sir, to the purpose.

KING LEAR
Who put my man i' the stocks?

Tucket within

CORNWALL

---

*she gave me dirty looks, attacked me with her tongue,
like a snake, going for the heart:
may all the vengeance heaven has saved up
fall on her ungrateful head! You infecting winds,
strike her young bones down with lameness!*

Come on now sir, come on!

*You quick lightning, stab your blinding fire
into her scornful eyes! You mists from the fens,
pulled up by the powerful sun, infect her beauty,
knock her down and ruin her pride!*

*Oh by the gods! This is how you will curse me,
when you get angry.*

*No, Regan, I will never curse you:
your womanly nature will never
make you so harsh: her eyes are fierce; but yours
comfort rather than burn. You would not
begrudge me my pleasures, reduce my retinue,
speak rudely to me, cut my rations,
and in the end bolt the doors
to my entrance: you are more respectful
of the duties of nature, of a child,
the function of manners, the gratitude that is
owed; you have not forgotten that I
gave you half my kingdom.*

Good sir, let's get to the point.

Who put my man in the stocks?

What trumpet's that?

REGAN
I know't, my sister's: this approves her letter,
That she would soon be here.

Enter OSWALD
Is your lady come?

KING LEAR
This is a slave, whose easy-borrow'd pride
Dwells in the fickle grace of her he follows.
Out, varlet, from my sight!

CORNWALL
What means your grace?

KING LEAR
Who stock'd my servant? Regan, I have good hope
Thou didst not know on't. Who comes here? O heavens,

Enter GONERIL
If you do love old men, if your sweet sway
Allow obedience, if yourselves are old,
Make it your cause; send down, and take my part!

To GONERIL
Art not ashamed to look upon this beard?
O Regan, wilt thou take her by the hand?

GONERIL
Why not by the hand, sir? How have I offended?
All's not offence that indiscretion finds
And dotage terms so.

KING LEAR
O sides, you are too tough;
Will you yet hold? How came my man i' the stocks?

CORNWALL
I set him there, sir: but his own disorders
Deserved much less advancement.

What's that trumpet?

I know it, it is my sister's. This confirms her letter, which said she would soon be here.

Has your lady come?

This man is scum, who lounges around basking in the reflected glory of the one he follows. Get out of my sight, you scoundrel!

What does your grace mean?

Who put my servant in the stocks? Regan, I'm assuming you knew nothing about it. Who's this coming? Good heavens,

If you love old men, if your sweet influence rewards obedience, if you are old yourself, then fight this battle; send down your powers for me.

Are you not ashamed to look at my beard? Oh Regan, you're taking her by the hand?

Why not by the hand, sir? What have I done wrong? Not everything is an offence just because rashness and senility say it is.

I feel like my heart is about to burst. Who put my man in the stocks?

I put him there, sir: but his behaviour deserved much worse.

KING LEAR
You! did you?

REGAN
I pray you, father, being weak, seem so.
If, till the expiration of your month,
You will return and sojourn with my sister,
Dismissing half your train, come then to me:
I am now from home, and out of that provision
Which shall be needful for your entertainment.

KING LEAR
Return to her, and fifty men dismiss'd?
No, rather I abjure all roofs, and choose
To wage against the enmity o' the air;
To be a comrade with the wolf and owl,--
Necessity's sharp pinch! Return with her?
Why, the hot-blooded France, that dowerless took
Our youngest born, I could as well be brought
To knee his throne, and, squire-like; pension beg
To keep base life afoot. Return with her?
Persuade me rather to be slave and sumpter
To this detested groom.

Pointing at OSWALD

GONERIL
At your choice, sir.

KING LEAR
I prithee, daughter, do not make me mad:
I will not trouble thee, my child; farewell:
We'll no more meet, no more see one another:
But yet thou art my flesh, my blood, my daughter;
Or rather a disease that's in my flesh,
Which I must needs call mine: thou art a boil,
A plague-sore, an embossed carbuncle,
In my corrupted blood. But I'll not chide thee;
Let shame come when it will, I do not call it:
I do not bid the thunder-bearer shoot,
Nor tell tales of thee to high-judging Jove:
Mend when thou canst; be better at thy leisure:
I can be patient; I can stay with Regan,

You! It was you?

I must ask you, father, to behave appropriately for your position. If you will go back, until the end of the month, and complete your stay with my sister, and dismiss half your entourage, them come to me: I am not at home now, and things are not prepared to give you a proper welcome.

Go back to her, and sack fifty men? No, in preference I reject all shelter and choose to live in the open air; I shall live with the wolf and the owl, if that's what I'm forced to do! Go back with her? I might just as well go to passionate France, who took my youngest child without a dowry, and kneel before his throne like a squire, begging for a pension to keep my poor life going. Go back with her? You might as well tell me that I had to be a servant and carrier for this disgusting groom.

It's your choice, sir.

Please, daughter, do not make me angry: I won't bother you, my child; farewell: we'll never meet or see one another again: but you are still my flesh and blood, my daughter: or rather you are a disease in my flesh, which I have to call mine: you are a boil a plague sore, a swollen carbuncle in my diseased blood. But I won't criticise you; let the shame come in its own time, I don't summon it: I have not told the God of Thunder to fire and I do not tell tales about you to the great judge Jove: change your ways when you can; get better at your own pace:

74

I and my hundred knights.

REGAN
Not altogether so:
I look'd not for you yet, nor am provided
For your fit welcome. Give ear, sir, to my sister;
For those that mingle reason with your passion
Must be content to think you old, and so--
But she knows what she does.

KING LEAR
Is this well spoken?

REGAN
I dare avouch it, sir: what, fifty followers?
Is it not well? What should you need of more?
Yea, or so many, sith that both charge and danger
Speak 'gainst so great a number? How, in one house,
Should many people, under two commands,
Hold amity? 'Tis hard; almost impossible.

GONERIL
Why might not you, my lord, receive attendance
From those that she calls servants or from mine?

REGAN
Why not, my lord? If then they chanced to slack you,
We could control them. If you will come to me,-
For now I spy a danger,--I entreat you
To bring but five and twenty: to no more
Will I give place or notice.

KING LEAR
I gave you all--

REGAN
And in good time you gave it.

KING LEAR
Made you my guardians, my depositaries;
But kept a reservation to be follow'd
With such a number. What, must I come to you
With five and twenty, Regan? said you so?

I can be patient; I can stay with Regan, me and my hundred knights.

That's not quite the case: I wasn't expecting you yet, and I'm not ready to give you a proper welcome. Listen, sir, to my sister; those who apply a little common sense to your anger must acknowledge that you are old, and so– but she knows what she's doing.

This is what you have to say?

It's what I think, sir: what, fifty followers? Isn't that enough? Why should you need any more? In fact why do you need so many, since the expense and risk suggest you should have fewer? How can so many people keep the peace in one house when they are under two different commanders? It's hard; it's almost impossible.

My lord, why can you not be waited on by her servants or by mine?

Why not, my lord? If they did not serve you well, we would punish them. If you want to come to me– because I now feel uneasy–I must ask you to only bring twenty-five: I will not accommodate any more than that.

I gave you everything–

At the right time.

I made you my stewardesses, my trustees; and all I asked was that I should have an entourage of a certain size. So, I have to come to you with twenty-five, Regan? Is that what you said?

REGAN
And speak't again, my lord; no more with me.

KING LEAR
Those wicked creatures yet do look well-favour'd,
When others are more wicked: not being the worst
Stands in some rank of praise.

To GONERIL
I'll go with thee:
Thy fifty yet doth double five and twenty,
And thou art twice her love.

GONERIL
Hear me, my lord;
What need you five and twenty, ten, or five,
To follow in a house where twice so many
Have a command to tend you?

REGAN
What need one?

KING LEAR
O, reason not the need: our basest beggars
Are in the poorest thing superfluous:
Allow not nature more than nature needs,
Man's life's as cheap as beast's: thou art a lady;
If only to go warm were gorgeous,
Why, nature needs not what thou gorgeous wear'st,
Which scarcely keeps thee warm. But, for true need,--
You heavens, give me that patience, patience I need!
You see me here, you gods, a poor old man,
As full of grief as age; wretched in both!
If it be you that stir these daughters' hearts
Against their father, fool me not so much
To bear it tamely; touch me with noble anger,
And let not women's weapons, water-drops,
Stain my man's cheeks! No, you unnatural hags,
I will have such revenges on you both,
That all the world shall--I will do such things,--

And I'll say it again, my lord; that's all I'll have.

These wicked creatures are still pretty, and there are others who are more wicked: I suppose not being the worst is something.

I'll go with you: your fifty is at least double her twenty-five, and you love me twice as much.

Listen to me, my lord; why do you need twenty five, ten, or five, to go with you to a house where twice that number have been ordered to serve you?

Why do you even need one?

Oh! Do not argue about need; our lowest beggars might have some small thing that is more than they need: if you don't think human nature needs more than the animals then a man's life is as cheap as an animal's. You are a lady; if being gorgeous just meant being warm, then nature would not need those gorgeous things you're wearing, which hardly keep you warm. But, for real need–
heavens, give me patience, patience is what I need!–
You gods see me here, the poor old man, as full of grief as he is of age, and made wretched by both! If it's you that has turned these daughters' hearts against their father, don't make me such a fool as to take it meekly; give me noble anger, and don't let women's weapons, teardrops, stain my manly cheeks! No, you unnatural hags, I will have such revenge on both of you that all the world shall–I will do

What they are, yet I know not: but they shall be
The terrors of the earth. You think I'll weep
No, I'll not weep:
I have full cause of weeping; but this heart
Shall break into a hundred thousand flaws,
Or ere I'll weep. O fool, I shall go mad!

such things, what they are I don't know yet, but they will be the worse things on earth. You think I'll cry; I will not:
I have every reason to, but this heart will shatter into a hundred thousand fragments before I'll cry. O fool! I shall go mad.

Exeunt KING LEAR, GLOUCESTER, KENT, and Fool

Storm and tempest

CORNWALL
Let us withdraw; 'twill be a storm.

Let's go inside, there's a storm coming.

REGAN
This house is little: the old man and his people
Cannot be well bestow'd.

This house is small: the old man and his servants can't be easily accommodated.

GONERIL
'Tis his own blame; hath put himself from rest,
And must needs taste his folly.

That's his own fault; he's taken himself away from shelter,
and he must face the consequences.

REGAN
For his particular, I'll receive him gladly,
But not one follower.

As an individual, I will gladly welcome him, but not one follower.

GONERIL
So am I purposed.
Where is my lord of Gloucester?

The same for me.
Where is my lord of Gloucester?

CORNWALL
Follow'd the old man forth: he is return'd.

He followed the old man out: here he is back.

Re-enter GLOUCESTER

GLOUCESTER
The king is in high rage.

The King is very angry.

CORNWALL
Whither is he going?

Where's he going?

GLOUCESTER
He calls to horse; but will I know not whither.

He's called for his horses, but I don't know where he means to go.

CORNWALL
'Tis best to give him way; he leads himself.

Let him go where he wants, he always wants his

77

GONERIL
My lord, entreat him by no means to stay.

GLOUCESTER
Alack, the night comes on, and the bleak winds
Do sorely ruffle; for many miles about
There's scarce a bush.

REGAN
O, sir, to wilful men,
The injuries that they themselves procure
Must be their schoolmasters. Shut up your doors:
He is attended with a desperate train;
And what they may incense him to, being apt
To have his ear abused, wisdom bids fear.

CORNWALL
Shut up your doors, my lord; 'tis a wild night:
My Regan counsels well; come out o' the storm.

Exeunt

own way.

My lord, on no account are you to beg him to stay.

Alas, night is falling, and the harsh winds are blowing strong; there is no shelter for many miles around.

Oh, sir, obstinate men have to learn from the injuries they inflict on themselves. Close your doors: his men are desperate; it would be wise to be cautious about what they might incite him to do, as he is so used to them leading him astray.

Close your doors, my lord; it's a wild night: my Regan gives good advice; come out of the storm.

Act 3

SCENE I. A heath.

Storm still. Enter KENT and a Gentleman, meeting

KENT
Who's there, besides foul weather?

Who's there, besides the foul weather?

Gentleman
One minded like the weather, most unquietly.

Someone who is feeling like the weather, very unsettled.

KENT
I know you. Where's the king?

I know you. Where's the King?

Gentleman
Contending with the fretful element:
Bids the winds blow the earth into the sea,
Or swell the curled water 'bove the main,
That things might change or cease; tears his white hair,
Which the impetuous blasts, with eyeless rage,
Catch in their fury, and make nothing of;
Strives in his little world of man to out-storm
The to-and-fro-conflicting wind and rain.
This night, wherein the cub-drawn bear would couch,
The lion and the belly-pinched wolf
Keep their fur dry, unbonneted he runs,
And bids what will take all.

Out battling with the weather: he calls on the winds to blow the earth into the sea, or blast the waves over the land, so that things could change or end; he tears at his white hair, which the harsh gusts, with invisible rage, catch in their fury and show no respect for; he is trying in his little world of a man to out blow the swirling winds and rain. This night, when a ravenous bear would stay home, a lion and a starving wolf would keep their fur dry, he runs about bareheaded and shouts that the winner will take all.

KENT
But who is with him?

But who is with him?

Gentleman
None but the fool; who labours to out-jest
His heart-struck injuries.

Only the fool, who is trying to drive out his heartfelt injuries with jokes.

KENT
Sir, I do know you;
And dare, upon the warrant of my note,
Commend a dear thing to you. There is division,
Although as yet the face of it be cover'd
With mutual cunning, 'twixt Albany and Cornwall;
Who have--as who have not, that their great stars

Sir, I know you; and on the strength of that I dare to trust you with something important. Although at the moment it is covered up by their mutual cunning, there is a split between Albany and Cornwall; they have–as who hasn't, when they get so high–servants, who seem innocent,

Throned and set high?--servants, who seem no less,
Which are to France the spies and speculations
Intelligent of our state; what hath been seen,
Either in snuffs and packings of the dukes,
Or the hard rein which both of them have borne
Against the old kind king; or something deeper,
Whereof perchance these are but furnishings;
But, true it is, from France there comes a power
Into this scatter'd kingdom; who already,
Wise in our negligence, have secret feet
In some of our best ports, and are at point
To show their open banner. Now to you:
If on my credit you dare build so far
To make your speed to Dover, you shall find
Some that will thank you, making just report
Of how unnatural and bemadding sorrow
The king hath cause to plain.
I am a gentleman of blood and breeding;
And, from some knowledge and assurance, offer
This office to you.

Gentleman
I will talk further with you.

KENT
No, do not.
For confirmation that I am much more
Than my out-wall, open this purse, and take
What it contains. If you shall see Cordelia,--
As fear not but you shall,--show her this ring;
And she will tell you who your fellow is
That yet you do not know. Fie on this storm!
I will go seek the king.

Gentleman
Give me your hand: have you no more to say?

KENT
Few words, but, to effect, more than all yet;
That, when we have found the king,--in which your pain
That way, I'll this,--he that first lights on him
Holla the other.

Exeunt severally

who are spies for France who give him information about our country. What has been seen either in the arguments and plots of the Dukes or the hard line which both of them have taken against the kind old King; or maybe something deeper, of which these things are just the pretexts– whatever it is it is certain that an army from France is coming into this divided kingdom; already, knowing of our negligence, they have gained a secret foothold in some of our best ports, and are about to come into the open. Now, as this relates to you: if you trust me enough to hurry to Dover, you will find some who will thank you for making a true report of how the King has reason to complain of unnatural and maddening sorrows. I am a gentleman of good blood and breeding, and I ask you to do this knowing that I can promise that what I say is true.

I want to talk more with you.

*No, do not.
To show you that I am much more than I appear, open this purse, and take out the contents. If you see Cordelia– as you certainly will–show her this ring; she will tell you who your comrade is that you don't know yet. Damn this storm! I will go and find the King.*

Give me your hand: have you nothing else to say?

Just a few words, but more important than all the others; that when we have found the King–you search in that direction I'll go this–the first one to find him should call the other.

SCENE II. Another part of the heath. Storm still.

Enter KING LEAR and Fool

KING LEAR
Blow, winds, and crack your cheeks! rage! blow!
You cataracts and hurricanoes, spout
Till you have drench'd our steeples, drown'd the cocks!
You sulphurous and thought-executing fires,
Vaunt-couriers to oak-cleaving thunderbolts,
Singe my white head! And thou, all-shaking thunder,
Smite flat the thick rotundity o' the world!
Crack nature's moulds, an germens spill at once,
That make ingrateful man!

Blow, winds, and burst your cheeks! Rage! Blow!
You floods and hurricanes, pour until you have soaked our steeples, drowned the weathercocks!
You sulphurous fires, coming at heaven's orders, forerunners of oak splitting thunder,
Burn my white head! And you, all shaking thunder,
smash the thick round world flat!
Crack the moulds and destroy all the seeds that nature uses to make ungrateful man.

Fool
O nuncle, court holy-water in a dry
house is better than this rain-water out o' door.
Good nuncle, in, and ask thy daughters' blessing:
here's a night pities neither wise man nor fool.

Oh nuncle, having to be flattering in a dry house is better than getting soaked out here. Good nuncle, let's go in and ask for your daughters' blessing:
this night won't spare the wise man or the fool.

KING LEAR
Rumble thy bellyful! Spit, fire! spout, rain!
Nor rain, wind, thunder, fire, are my daughters:
I tax not you, you elements, with unkindness;
I never gave you kingdom, call'd you children,
You owe me no subscription: then let fall
Your horrible pleasure: here I stand, your slave,
A poor, infirm, weak, and despised old man:
But yet I call you servile ministers,
That have with two pernicious daughters join'd
Your high engender'd battles 'gainst a head
So old and white as this. O! O! 'tis foul!

Rumble to your heart's content! Spit, fire! Spout, rain! Rain, wind, thunder, nor fire, are not my daughters: I don't charge you, elements, with unkindness; I never gave you a kingdom, called you my children, you owe me nothing: let your horrible course run free: here I stand, your slave, a poor, infirm, weak and despised old man: I call you serving agents, joining with two wicked daughters in your heavenly attacks on a head as old and white as this. Oh ho! It's terrible.

Fool
He that has a house to put's head in has a good head-piece.
The cod-piece that will house
Before the head has any,
The head and he shall louse;
So beggars marry many.

The one with a roof over his head has a good hat.
Someone who sleeps with a woman before he has a roof
will end up married, sharing her lice;
so beggars marry many.

The man that makes his toe What he his heart should make Shall of a corn cry woe, And turn his sleep to wake. For there was never yet fair woman but she made mouths in a glass.	The man who thinks his toe is as important as his heart will get sorrow from a corn and that will keep him awake. I never saw a beautiful woman yet who didn't make faces in the mirror.

KING LEAR
No, I will be the pattern of all patience;
I will say nothing.

No, I will be a perfect example of patience;
I will say nothing.

Enter KENT

KENT
Who's there?

Who's there?

Fool
Marry, here's grace and a cod-piece; that's a wise
man and a fool.

Here's a king and a codpiece; I mean a wise
man and a fool.

KENT
Alas, sir, are you here? things that love night
Love not such nights as these; the wrathful skies
Gallow the very wanderers of the dark,
And make them keep their caves: since I was man,
Such sheets of fire, such bursts of horrid thunder,
Such groans of roaring wind and rain, I never
Remember to have heard: man's nature cannot carry
The affliction nor the fear.

Alas, sir, are you here? Even things that love the night
don't like nights like these; the angry skies
terrify the beasts of the dark,
and make them stay in their caves: since I became a man
I can never remember such flashing lightning,
such horrid bursts of thunder, such groans
of roaring wind and rain: a man cannot bear
the pain or the fear.

KING LEAR
Let the great gods,
That keep this dreadful pother o'er our heads,
Find out their enemies now. Tremble, thou wretch,
That hast within thee undivulged crimes,
Unwhipp'd of justice: hide thee, thou bloody hand;
Thou perjured, and thou simular man of virtue
That art incestuous: caitiff, to pieces shake,
That under covert and convenient seeming

Let the great gods,
that are causing this terrible row over our
heads, find out who their enemies are now.
Anyone who has secret crimes within them
which have gone unpunished
should tremble now: hide your bloody hands
you perjurer, and you, the same type who is
incestuous; you wretch, shake yourself to pieces,
who with secret and silky hypocrisy
has plotted against a man's life; may your secret

83

Hast practised on man's life: close pent-up guilts,
Rive your concealing continents, and cry
These dreadful summoners grace. I am a man
More sinn'd against than sinning.

KENT
Alack, bare-headed!
Gracious my lord, hard by here is a hovel;
Some friendship will it lend you 'gainst the tempest:
Repose you there; while I to this hard house--
More harder than the stones whereof 'tis raised;
Which even but now, demanding after you,
Denied me to come in--return, and force
Their scanted courtesy.

KING LEAR
My wits begin to turn.
Come on, my boy: how dost, my boy? art cold?
I am cold myself. Where is this straw, my fellow?
The art of our necessities is strange,
That can make vile things precious. Come, your hovel.
Poor fool and knave, I have one part in my heart
That's sorry yet for thee.

Fool
[Singing]
He that has and a little tiny wit--
With hey, ho, the wind and the rain,--
Must make content with his fortunes fit,
For the rain it raineth every day.

KING LEAR
True, my good boy. Come, bring us to this hovel.

Exeunt KING LEAR and KENT

Fool
This is a brave night to cool a courtezan.
I'll speak a prophecy ere I go:
When priests are more in word than matter;

guilt burst through your disguise and make you beg these dreadful judges for mercy. I am a man who is more sinned against than sinning.

Dear me, bare headed!
My gracious lord, there is a shack nearby; it will give you some protection against the storm: you rest there, while I go to this hard house–even harder than the stones it is made of; even just now, when I asked after you, they would not let me in–again and force them to show us some courtesy.

I'm beginning to go mad.
Come on, my boy: how are you, my boy? Are you cold?
I am cold myself. Where is this place, my friend? Necessity is a strange master, which makes vile things valuable. Come on, show me your shack.
Poor fool and knave, one part of my heart is still sorry for you.

The one who has a tiny mind–
sing hey, ho, the wind and the rain–
must be happy with whatever he gets, for the rain comes down every day.

That's true, my good lad. Come on, bring us to this shack.

This night would cool a harlot's ardour.
I'll make a prediction before I go: when priests are more about speech than

84

When brewers mar their malt with water;	substance, when brewers water down their beer,
When nobles are their tailors' tutors;	when noblemen start teaching tailors,
No heretics burn'd, but wenches' suitors;	when heretics aren't burned but boyfriends are,
When every case in law is right;	when every legal case is just,
No squire in debt, nor no poor knight;	when no squires or poor knights are in debt,
When slanders do not live in tongues;	when nobody tells lies,
Nor cutpurses come not to throngs;	and pickpockets don't come to crowds,
When usurers tell their gold i' the field;	when moneylenders count their gold in fields,
And bawds and whores do churches build;	and pimps and whores build churches,
Then shall the realm of Albion	then the Kingdom of England
Come to great confusion:	will be in great turmoil:
Then comes the time, who lives to see't,	for those who live to see that time,
That going shall be used with feet.	they'll find all men will have to walk.
This prophecy Merlin shall make; for I live before his time.	Merlin will make this prophecy because I was born before him.

Exit

SCENE III. Gloucester's castle.

Enter GLOUCESTER and EDMUND

GLOUCESTER
Alack, alack, Edmund, I like not this unnatural
dealing. When I desire their leave that I might
pity him, they took from me the use of mine
own
house; charged me, on pain of their perpetual
displeasure, neither to speak of him, entreat for
him, nor any way sustain him.

EDMUND
Most savage and unnatural!

GLOUCESTER
Go to; say you nothing. There's a division
betwixt
the dukes; and a worse matter than that: I have
received a letter this night; 'tis dangerous to be
spoken; I have locked the letter in my closet:
these injuries the king now bears will be
revenged
home; there's part of a power already footed: we
must incline to the king. I will seek him, and
privily relieve him: go you and maintain talk
with
the duke, that my charity be not of him
perceived:
if he ask for me. I am ill, and gone to bed.
Though I die for it, as no less is threatened me,
the king my old master must be relieved. There
is
some strange thing toward, Edmund; pray you,
be careful.

Exit

EDMUND
This courtesy, forbid thee, shall the duke
Instantly know; and of that letter too:
This seems a fair deserving, and must draw me
That which my father loses; no less than all:
The younger rises when the old doth fall.

*Alas, alas, Edmund, I don't like this unnatural
behaviour. When I asked their permission
to pity him, they took away the use of my own
house; they ordered me, on pain of their
permanent
hatred, not to speak of him, plead for him,
nor in any way to help him.*

This is most savage and unnatural!

*And that's not the half of it. There is a split
between
the Dukes, and there's something worse going
on. I have
received a letter tonight; it is dangerous
to speak of; I have locked the letter in my room.
These
injuries done to the King will come home to
roost;
part of an army has already landed; we must
support the King. I will find him and secretly
help him; you go and talk to the Duke,
so that he does not discover my charity. If he
asks for me
say that I am ill and have gone to bed. Even if I
die for it, as they
threaten I will, I must still help the King, my old
master.
There are strange things going on, Edmund;
please, be careful.*

*The Duke shall instantly know of this charity,
which you were forbidden to do; he'll know
about that letter too: that would seem to deserve
a reward, and must give me a chance of getting
the things taken from my father; I want it all:*

the young one rises as the old one falls.

Exit

SCENE IV. The heath. Before a hovel.

Enter KING LEAR, KENT, and Fool

KENT
Here is the place, my lord; good my lord, enter:
The tyranny of the open night's too rough
For nature to endure.

This is the place, my lord; come in my good lord: the night is too rough to stay in the open.

Storm still

KING LEAR
Let me alone.

Leave me alone.

KENT
Good my lord, enter here.

My good lord, come in.

KING LEAR
Wilt break my heart?

Do you want to break my heart?

KENT
I had rather break mine own. Good my lord, enter.

I would rather break my own. My good lord, come in.

KING LEAR
Thou think'st 'tis much that this contentious storm
Invades us to the skin: so 'tis to thee;
But where the greater malady is fix'd,
The lesser is scarce felt. Thou'ldst shun a bear;
But if thy flight lay toward the raging sea,
Thou'ldst meet the bear i' the mouth. When the mind's free,
The body's delicate: the tempest in my mind
Doth from my senses take all feeling else
Save what beats there. Filial ingratitude!
Is it not as this mouth should tear this hand
For lifting food to't? But I will punish home:
No, I will weep no more. In such a night
To shut me out! Pour on; I will endure.
In such a night as this! O Regan, Goneril!
Your old kind father, whose frank heart gave all,--
O, that way madness lies; let me shun that;
No more of that.

*It bothers you that this terrible storm soaks us to the skin: it bothers you; but when there is a greater illness, one hardly feels the lesser one. You would run from a bear; but if your escape route took you into the raging sea, you would fight that bear face-to-face. When your mind is at ease the body is sensitive; the storm in my mind takes away all other feelings except what is in there–the ingratitude of my daughters!
Should the mouth bite the hand that feeds it? But I will have my revenge:
no, I will not cry any more. To lock me out on such a night? Carry on raining, I will endure it. On a night like this? O Regan, Goneril! Your kind old father, whose open heart gave you everything–
oh! Thinking like that leads to madness; I reject that; no more of that.*

88

KENT
Good my lord, enter here.

My good lord, please come in.

KING LEAR
Prithee, go in thyself: seek thine own ease:
This tempest will not give me leave to ponder
On things would hurt me more. But I'll go in.

Please, go in yourself: make yourself comfortable: this storm stops me from thinking about other things which are more painful. But I'll go in.

To the Fool
In, boy; go first. You houseless poverty,--
Nay, get thee in. I'll pray, and then I'll sleep.

You go in first, boy. You poor homeless— no, go inside. I'll pray, and then I'll sleep.

Fool goes in
Poor naked wretches, whereso'er you are,
That bide the pelting of this pitiless storm,
How shall your houseless heads and unfed sides,
Your loop'd and window'd raggedness, defend you
From seasons such as these? O, I have ta'en
Too little care of this! Take physic, pomp;
Expose thyself to feel what wretches feel,
That thou mayst shake the superflux to them,
And show the heavens more just.

Poor naked wretches, wherever you are, that suffer the pelting of this pitiless storm, how will your roofless heads and hungry sides, with your clothes full of holes, defend you against this sort of weather? Oh! I have paid too little attention to this. It would do you good, rich ones; exposing yourself to what poor men feel, you might then give them some of your surplus to show that heaven is more fair.

EDGAR
[Within] Fathom and half, fathom and half! Poor Tom!

Fathom and half, fathom and half! Poor Tom!

The Fool runs out from the hovel

Fool
Come not in here, nuncle, here's a spirit.
Help me, help me!

Don't come in here, nuncle, there's a ghost. Help me, help me!

KENT
Give me thy hand. Who's there?

Give me your hand. Who's there?

Fool
A spirit, a spirit: he says his name's poor Tom.

A ghost, a ghost: he says his name is poor Tom.

KENT
What art thou that dost grumble there i' the straw?
Come forth.

Who are you, muttering there in the straw? Come out.

Enter EDGAR disguised as a mad man

EDGAR
Away! the foul fiend follows me!
Through the sharp hawthorn blows the cold wind.
Hum! go to thy cold bed, and warm thee.

KING LEAR
Hast thou given all to thy two daughters?
And art thou come to this?

EDGAR
Who gives any thing to poor Tom? whom the foul
fiend hath led through fire and through flame, and
through ford and whirlipool e'er bog and quagmire;
that hath laid knives under his pillow, and halters
in his pew; set ratsbane by his porridge; made him
proud of heart, to ride on a bay trotting-horse over
four-inched bridges, to course his own shadow for a
traitor. Bless thy five wits! Tom's a-cold,--O, do de, do de, do de. Bless thee from whirlwinds,
star-blasting, and taking! Do poor Tom some
charity, whom the foul fiend vexes: there could I
have him now,--and there,--and there again, and
there.

*Go away! The devil is chasing me!
The cold wind blows through the sharp hawthorn bushes.
Hum! Go to your cold bed and warm up.*

Have you given everything to your two daughters? And has it brought you to this?

*Who gives anything to poor Tom? The one the Devil has led through the fire and the flame, through the ford and the whirlpool, bog and swamp;
he has put knives under his pillow, nooses outside his bedroom window; put rat poison by his porridge,
made him so cocky that he would ride his trotting horse
over four inch bridges, hunting his own shadow as a traitor.
Bless your five wits! Tom's cold. Oh! La di da di da. Save you from whirlwinds, lightning and illness! Be nice to poor Tom, whom the devil tortures. I could get him now, there, there again, there.*

Storm still

KING LEAR
What, have his daughters brought him to this pass?
Couldst thou save nothing? Didst thou give them all?

*What, have his daughters reduced him to this state?
Couldn't you save anything? Did you give them the lot?*

Fool
Nay, he reserved a blanket, else we had been all shamed.

No, he's saved a blanket, otherwise we'd all be embarrassed.

KING LEAR

Now, all the plagues that in the pendulous air
Hang fated o'er men's faults light on thy
daughters!

KENT
He hath no daughters, sir.

KING LEAR
Death, traitor! nothing could have subdued nature
To such a lowness but his unkind daughters.
Is it the fashion, that discarded fathers
Should have thus little mercy on their flesh?
Judicious punishment! 'twas this flesh begot
Those pelican daughters.

EDGAR
Pillicock sat on Pillicock-hill:
Halloo, halloo, loo, loo!

Fool
This cold night will turn us all to fools and madmen.

EDGAR
Take heed o' the foul fiend: obey thy parents;
keep thy word justly; swear not; commit not with
man's sworn spouse; set not thy sweet heart on proud
array. Tom's a-cold.

KING LEAR
What hast thou been?

EDGAR
A serving-man, proud in heart and mind; that curled
my hair; wore gloves in my cap; served the lust of
my mistress' heart, and did the act of darkness with
her; swore as many oaths as I spake words, and
broke them in the sweet face of heaven: one that
slept in the contriving of lust, and waked to do it:

Now, may all the plagues that hang in the air waiting to punish men's faults crash down on your daughters!

He has no daughters, sir.

*Death to you, traitor! Nothing could have brought someone
so low except for unkind daughters.
Is this the fashion, for rejected fathers
to punish their flesh like this?
An appropriate punishment! It was the flesh that created those cannibal daughters.*

*Pillicock sat on Pillicock-hill:
Halloo, halloo, loo, loo!*

This cold night will turn us all into fools and madmen.

Listen to the devil: obey your parents; always keep your word; do not swear; don't commit adultery; don't yearn for flashy clothes. Tom's cold.

What were you?

*A suitor, proud in heart and mind; I curled my hair, wore gloves in my cap, satisfied the lust in my mistress' heart, and did the forbidden
act with her; I swore as many oaths as I spoke words
and broke them right in front of God. I would plot
my seductions in my sleep, then carry them out when I woke. I loved*

wine loved I deeply, dice dearly: and in woman
out-paramoured the Turk: false of heart, light of
ear, bloody of hand; hog in sloth, fox in stealth,
wolf in greediness, dog in madness, lion in prey.
Let not the creaking of shoes nor the rustling of
silks betray thy poor heart to woman: keep thy foot
out of brothels, thy hand out of plackets, thy pen
from lenders' books, and defy the foul fiend.
Still through the hawthorn blows the cold wind:
Says suum, mun, ha, no, nonny.
Dolphin my boy, my boy, sessa! let him trot by.

wine deeply, dice dearly, and as for women I had more than a sultan: I had a false heart, I listened to all gossip, I had blood on my hands; I was a pig for laziness, a fox for cunning, a wolf for greed, a dog for madness, a lion for hunting. Don't let women trap your poor heart with their creaking shoes and their rustling silks: keep your foot out of brothels, your hand out of petticoats, your pen out of moneylenders' ledgers, and defy the devil. The cold wind still blows through the hawthorn, says suum, mun, ha, no, nonny. Dolphin my boy, my boy, sessa! let him trot by.

Storm still

KING LEAR
Why, thou wert better in thy grave than to answer
with thy uncovered body this extremity of the skies.
Is man no more than this? Consider him well. Thou
owest the worm no silk, the beast no hide, the sheep
no wool, the cat no perfume. Ha! here's three on
's are sophisticated! Thou art the thing itself:
unaccommodated man is no more but such a poor bare,
forked animal as thou art. Off, off, you lendings!
come unbutton here.

You would be better off in the grave than exposing your uncovered body to the extremes of the weather. Is this all that man is? Look at him carefully. You don't owe the worm any silk, the animal no skin, the sheep no wool, the cat no perfume. Ha! We three have been corrupted! You are the genuine article: natural man is nothing more than such a poor bare two legged creature like you. Off, off, you borrowed things! Let's undo these buttons.

Tearing off his clothes

Fool
Prithee, nuncle, be contented; 'tis a naughty night
to swim in. Now a little fire in a wild field were
like an old lecher's heart; a small spark, all the
rest on's body cold. Look, here comes a walking fire.

Please, nuncle, be easy; this is a bad night for swimming. A little fire in a big field is like an old lecher's heart; a little spark in a great coldness. Look, here comes a walking flame.

Enter GLOUCESTER, with a torch

EDGAR
This is the foul fiend Flibbertigibbet: he begins

This is the foul devil Flibbertigibbet: he starts

92

at curfew, and walks till the first cock; he gives the web and the pin, squints the eye, and makes the
hare-lip; mildews the white wheat, and hurts the poor creature of earth.
S. Withold footed thrice the old;
He met the night-mare, and her nine-fold;
Bid her alight,
And her troth plight,
And, aroint thee, witch, aroint thee!

	at the curfew and walks until midnight; he gives people cataracts, squints and hare lips; he puts mildew in the young wheat, and hurts all poor creatures. St Withold subdued the demon three times; he met the demon and her nine offspring; he told her to get down and make a promise and then he banished the witch.

KENT
How fares your grace?

How is your Grace?

KING LEAR
What's he?

Who's that?

KENT
Who's there? What is't you seek?

Who's there? What you want?

GLOUCESTER
What are you there? Your names?

Who are you? What are your names?

EDGAR
Poor Tom; that eats the swimming frog, the toad,
the tadpole, the wall-newt and the water; that in the fury of his heart, when the foul fiend rages, eats cow-dung for sallets; swallows the old rat and
the ditch-dog; drinks the green mantle of the standing pool; who is whipped from tithing to tithing, and stock- punished, and imprisoned; who
hath had three suits to his back, six shirts to his body, horse to ride, and weapon to wear;
But mice and rats, and such small deer,
Have been Tom's food for seven long year.
Beware my follower. Peace, Smulkin; peace, thou fiend!

Poor Tom; the one who eats the swimming frog, the toad, the tadpole, the water newt and the lizard; who in his madness, when the devil rages, eats cow-dung instead of salad; he swallows the old rat and dead dogs; he drinks the scum off the standing pool; he is whipped from parish to parish, put in the stocks and imprisoned; he once had three suits and six shirts to wear, a horse to ride and a weapon to carry; but mice and rats and such small game have been Tom's food for seven long years. Watch out for the devil. Peace, Smulkin, peace you devil!

GLOUCESTER
What, hath your grace no better company?

Is this the best company your Grace can get?

EDGAR
The prince of darkness is a gentleman:

The devil is a gentleman:

93

Modo he's call'd, and Mahu.

GLOUCESTER
Our flesh and blood is grown so vile, my lord,
That it doth hate what gets it.

EDGAR
Poor Tom's a-cold.

GLOUCESTER
Go in with me: my duty cannot suffer
To obey in all your daughters' hard commands:
Though their injunction be to bar my doors,
And let this tyrannous night take hold upon you,
Yet have I ventured to come seek you out,
And bring you where both fire and food is ready.

KING LEAR
First let me talk with this philosopher.
What is the cause of thunder?

KENT
Good my lord, take his offer; go into the house.

KING LEAR
I'll talk a word with this same learned Theban.
What is your study?

EDGAR
How to prevent the fiend, and to kill vermin.

KING LEAR
Let me ask you one word in private.

KENT
Importune him once more to go, my lord;
His wits begin to unsettle.

GLOUCESTER
Canst thou blame him?

Storm still
His daughters seek his death: ah, that good Kent!

he's called Modo, and Mahu.	
Our own flesh and blood has become so vile, my lord, that it despises its parents.	
Poor Tom's cold.	
Come in to my house: my loyalty will not allow me to obey all your daughters' harsh orders: though they have commanded me to lock my doors, and let this terrible night descend on you, I have decided to come and find you and bring you to where there is both food and a fire.	
Let me first talk with this philosopher. What causes thunder?	
My good lord, take him up on his offer; go into the house.	
I'll have a word with this clever chap. What's your speciality?	
How to block the devil, and to kill vermin.	
Let me have a word with you in private.	
Plead with him again to go in, my lord; he's beginning to go mad.	
Can you blame him?	
His daughters want him dead: ah, Kent was a good man!	

He said it would be thus, poor banish'd man!
Thou say'st the king grows mad; I'll tell thee, friend,
I am almost mad myself: I had a son,
Now outlaw'd from my blood; he sought my life,
But lately, very late: I loved him, friend;
No father his son dearer: truth to tell thee,
The grief hath crazed my wits. What a night's this!
I do beseech your grace,--

He said this would happen, the poor exile!
You say the King is going mad; I'll tell you my friend,
I am almost mad myself: I had a son,
whom I have now disowned; he wanted to kill me,
very recently: I loved him, my friend;
no father loved his son more dearly: to tell you the truth,
the grief has made me mad. What a night this is!
I beg your grace–

KING LEAR
O, cry your mercy, sir.
Noble philosopher, your company.

Oh, excuse me sir.
Noble philosopher, come to me.

EDGAR
Tom's a-cold.

Tom's cold.

GLOUCESTER
In, fellow, there, into the hovel: keep thee warm.

Go in, fellow, in there, into the shack: keep yourself warm.

KING LEAR
Come let's in all.

Come on, let's all go in.

KENT
This way, my lord.

This way, my lord.

KING LEAR
With him;
I will keep still with my philosopher.

You go with him;
I'll stay with this philosopher.

KENT
Good my lord, soothe him; let him take the fellow.

Humor him my good lord, let him bring the fellow.

GLOUCESTER
Take him you on.

You lead him in.

KENT
Sirrah, come on; go along with us.

Come on, sir, come with us.

KING LEAR
Come, good Athenian.

Come on, you clever fellow.

GLOUCESTER

95

No words, no words: hush.

EDGAR
Child Rowland to the dark tower came,
His word was still,--Fie, foh, and fum,
I smell the blood of a British man.

Exeunt

Say nothing, say nothing: hush

*Child Roland to the dark tower came,
His motto remained: Fee fie fo fum,
I smell the blood of a British man.*

SCENE V. Gloucester's castle.

Enter CORNWALL and EDMUND

CORNWALL
I will have my revenge ere I depart his house.

I will have my revenge before I leave his house.

EDMUND
How, my lord, I may be censured, that nature thus
gives way to loyalty, something fears me to think
of.

I worry, my lord, how I may be punished, for allowing loyalty to get the better of my natural instincts.

CORNWALL
I now perceive, it was not altogether your
brother's evil disposition made him seek his death;
but a provoking merit, set a-work by a reprovable
badness in himself.

I can now see that it was not just your brother's evil nature that made him want to kill your father; there was a good reason, though it was spurred on by his own wickedness.

EDMUND
How malicious is my fortune, that I must repent to
be just! This is the letter he spoke of, which
approves him an intelligent party to the advantages
of France: O heavens! that this treason were not, or not I the detector!

How unhappy my fortune is, that I must feel bad about doing the right thing! This is the letter he spoke of, which proves him to be a spy for France: Oh heavens! I wish this treason did not exist, or that I was not the one who discovered it.

CORNWALL
Go with me to the duchess.

We'll both go to the Duchess.

EDMUND
If the matter of this paper be certain, you have
mighty business in hand.

If what's in this paper is definitely right, you have great things to do.

CORNWALL
True or false, it hath made thee earl of
Gloucester. Seek out where thy father is, that he
may be ready for our apprehension.

True or false, it has made you Earl of Gloucester. Find out where your father is, so we can have him arrested.

EDMUND
[Aside] If I find him comforting the king, it will

If I find him assisting the King, it will

stuff his suspicion more fully.--[Aloud] I will persevere in
my course of loyalty, though the conflict be sore between that and my blood.

make him even more suspicious--I will continue my loyal efforts, even though it is almost tearing me apart.

CORNWALL
I will lay trust upon thee; and thou shalt find a dearer father in my love.

I will put my trust in you; and you will find a better father in me.

Exeunt

SCENE VI. A chamber in a farmhouse adjoining the castle.

Enter GLOUCESTER, KING LEAR, KENT, Fool, and EDGAR

GLOUCESTER
Here is better than the open air; take it thankfully. I will piece out the comfort with what
addition I can: I will not be long from you.

You're better off in here than in the open air; be grateful for it. I will bring what I can to make it more comfortable: I shan't be away for long.

KENT
All the power of his wits have given way to his impatience: the gods reward your kindness!

All his sense has given way to his impatience; may the gods reward you for your kindness!

Exit GLOUCESTER

EDGAR
Frateretto calls me; and tells me
Nero is an angler in the lake of darkness.
Pray, innocent, and beware the foul fiend.

Frateretto calls me, and tells me that Nero fishes in the lake of hell. Pray, you innocent, and beware of the devil.

Fool
Prithee, nuncle, tell me whether a madman be a gentleman or a yeoman?

Please, nuncle, can you tell me whether a madman is a gentleman or a commoner?

KING LEAR
A king, a king!

A King, a King!

Fool
No, he's a yeoman that has a gentleman to his son;
for he's a mad yeoman that sees his son a gentleman
before him.

*No, he's a commoner that has a gentleman as his son;
a commoner would have to be mad to let his son become a gentleman
before him.*

KING LEAR
To have a thousand with red burning spits
Come hissing in upon 'em,--

To have a thousand with red burning weapons hissing down on them—

EDGAR
The foul fiend bites my back.

The devil is biting my back.

Fool
He's mad that trusts in the tameness of a wolf, a horse's health, a boy's love, or a whore's oath.

A madman is one who trusts in the tameness of a wolf, the health of a horse, the love of a boy, or

KING LEAR
It shall be done; I will arraign them straight.

To EDGAR
Come, sit thou here, most learned justicer;

To the Fool
Thou, sapient sir, sit here. Now, you she foxes!

EDGAR
Look, where he stands and glares!
Wantest thou eyes at trial, madam?
Come o'er the bourn, Bessy, to me,--

Fool
Her boat hath a leak,
And she must not speak
Why she dares not come over to thee.

EDGAR
The foul fiend haunts poor Tom in the voice of a nightingale. Hopdance cries in Tom's belly for two
white herring. Croak not, black angel; I have no food for thee.

KENT
How do you, sir? Stand you not so amazed:
Will you lie down and rest upon the cushions?

KING LEAR
I'll see their trial first. Bring in the evidence.

To EDGAR
Thou robed man of justice, take thy place;

To the Fool
And thou, his yoke-fellow of equity,
Bench by his side:

To KENT
you are o' the commission,
Sit you too.

---

the promise of a whore.

It shall be done; I will put them on trial at once.

Come, you sit here, you learned judge.

You, you wise man, sit here. Now, you vixens!

*Look how the devil stands and glares!
Do you want witnesses to your trial, madam?
Come over the stream to me, Bessie—*

*Her boat has a leak,
and she must not say
why she doesn't dare come over to you.*

The devil haunts poor Tom with the voice of a nightingale. Hoppedance is in Tom's belly, pleading for two pickled herrings. Don't rumble, stomach; I have no food for you.

*How are you, sir? Don't stand there dumbfounded:
won't you lie down and rest on the cushions?*

I'll see their trial first. Bring in the evidence.

You robed judge, take your place;

*And you, his equal partner,
sit next to him on the bench:*

*you're one of the board,
you sit down too.*

100

EDGAR
Let us deal justly.
Sleepest or wakest thou, jolly shepherd?
Thy sheep be in the corn;
And for one blast of thy minikin mouth,
Thy sheep shall take no harm.
Pur! the cat is gray.

	Let us act with justice.
	Are you asleep or awake, Johnny Shepherd?
	Your sheep are in the cornfield;
	and for one song from you,
	your sheep will come to no harm.
	Purr! It's a grey cat.

KING LEAR
Arraign her first; 'tis Goneril. I here take my oath before this honourable assembly, she kicked the
poor king her father.

*Charge her first; it is Goneril. I will now swear in front of this honourable meeting, she kicked
the poor King her father.*

Fool
Come hither, mistress. Is your name Goneril?

Come here, lady. Is your name Goneril?

KING LEAR
She cannot deny it.

She can't deny it.

Fool
Cry you mercy, I took you for a joint-stool.

I beg your pardon, I thought you were a footstool.

KING LEAR
And here's another, whose warp'd looks proclaim
What store her heart is made on. Stop her there!
Arms, arms, sword, fire! Corruption in the place!
False justicer, why hast thou let her 'scape?

*And here's another one, whose twisted face shows
what she has in her heart. Stop her there!
Arms, arms, sword, fire! There is corruption here!
False judge, why have you let her escape?*

EDGAR
Bless thy five wits!

Bless your five wits!

KENT
O pity! Sir, where is the patience now,
That thou so oft have boasted to retain?

*I pity you! Sir, where is your temper now,
that you used to be so proud of keeping?*

EDGAR
[Aside] My tears begin to take his part so much,
They'll mar my counterfeiting.

*I begin to cry so much for him,
it'll give away my disguise.*

KING LEAR
The little dogs and all, Tray, Blanch, and
Sweet-heart, see, they bark at me.

*The little dogs and all, Tray, Blanch and
Sweetheart, look they bark at me.*

EDGAR
Tom will throw his head at them. Avaunt, you curs!
Be thy mouth or black or white,
Tooth that poisons if it bite;
Mastiff, grey-hound, mongrel grim,
Hound or spaniel, brach or lym,
Or bobtail tike or trundle-tail,
Tom will make them weep and wail:
For, with throwing thus my head,
Dogs leap the hatch, and all are fled.
Do de, de, de. Sessa! Come, march to wakes and fairs and market-towns. Poor Tom, thy horn is dry.

Tom will drive them off. Away, you curs! Whether your mouth is black or white the bite of your teeth is poison; mastiff, greyhound, grim mongrel, hound or spaniel, beagle or bloodhound, short or long tailed, Tom will make them weep and wail: for as I charge at them the dogs leap through the door, and they are all gone. Do, de, de, de. Off you go! Come, let's march to funerals fairs and market towns. Poor Tom, your glass is empty.

KING LEAR
Then let them anatomize Regan; see what breeds
about her heart. Is there any cause in nature that makes these hard hearts?

Then let them dissect Regan; let's see what her heart is made of. Is there anything in nature that causes these hard hearts?

To EDGAR
You, sir, I entertain for one of my hundred; only I
do not like the fashion of your garments: you will
say they are Persian attire: but let them be changed.

You, sir, I welcome as one of my knights; only I don't like the way you are dressed: you will say they are Persian clothes: but change them.

KENT
Now, good my lord, lie here and rest awhile.

Now, my good lord, lie here and rest for a while.

KING LEAR
Make no noise, make no noise; draw the curtains:
so, so, so. We'll go to supper i' he morning. So, so, so.

Keep quiet, keep quiet; draw the curtains: there, there, there. We'll go to supper in the morning. There, there, there.

Fool
And I'll go to bed at noon.

And I'll go to bed at noon.

Re-enter GLOUCESTER

GLOUCESTER
Come hither, friend: where is the king my

Come here, friend: where is my master the

master? | *King?*

KENT
Here, sir; but trouble him not, his wits are gone. | *Here, sir; but do not bother him, he's lost his mind.*

GLOUCESTER
Good friend, I prithee, take him in thy arms;
I have o'erheard a plot of death upon him:
There is a litter ready; lay him in 't,
And drive towards Dover, friend, where thou shalt meet
Both welcome and protection. Take up thy master:
If thou shouldst dally half an hour, his life,
With thine, and all that offer to defend him,
Stand in assured loss: take up, take up;
And follow me, that will to some provision
Give thee quick conduct.

*Please, good friend, pick him up in your arms;
I have overheard a plot to kill him:
I have a litter ready; put him in it
and drive towards Dover, friend, where you shall find
both welcome and protection. Pick up your master:
if you delay half an hour, his life,
and yours, and those of everyone who tries to defend him, will certainly be lost: pick him up, pick him up; and follow me, I will take you quickly to the things I have ready.*

KENT
Oppressed nature sleeps:
This rest might yet have balm'd thy broken senses,
Which, if convenience will not allow,
Stand in hard cure.

*His troubled soul sleeps:
this rest still might have healed your damaged mind,
which, if it hasn't happened now,
will be almost impossible to cure.*

To the Fool
Come, help to bear thy master;
Thou must not stay behind.

*Come on, help carry your master;
you mustn't stay behind.*

GLOUCESTER
Come, come, away.

Come on, come on, let's go.

Exeunt all but EDGAR

EDGAR
When we our betters see bearing our woes,
We scarcely think our miseries our foes.
Who alone suffers suffers most i' the mind,
Leaving free things and happy shows behind:
But then the mind much sufferance doth o'er skip,
When grief hath mates, and bearing fellowship.
How light and portable my pain seems now,
When that which makes me bend makes the king bow,

*When we see our betters enduring our sorrows,
we hardly think of our miseries as enemies.
The one who suffers alone suffers mostly in the mind,
forgetting carefree things and happy sights:
but the mind can cope with much suffering,
when grief has friends, and suffering is shared.
How light and bearable my pain now seems,
when the thing I suffer from is worse for the King,*

103

He childed as I father'd! Tom, away!
Mark the high noises; and thyself bewray,
When false opinion, whose wrong thought defiles thee,
In thy just proof, repeals and reconciles thee.
What will hap more to-night, safe 'scape the king!
Lurk, lurk.

Exit

he has cruel children as I have a cruel father! Tom, away! Look at the great events; throw off your disguise, when those who think wrongly of you can see the real evidence, repeal your sentence and reconcile you with your father. Whatever else happens tonight, may the king escape safely!
I'll hide and bide my time.

SCENE VII. Gloucester's castle.

Enter CORNWALL, REGAN, GONERIL, EDMUND, and Servants

CORNWALL
Post speedily to my lord your husband; show him
this letter: the army of France is landed. Seek out the villain Gloucester.

*Send quickly to my lord, your husband; show him
this letter: the French army has landed. Find the villain Gloucester.*

Exeunt some of the Servants

REGAN
Hang him instantly.

Hang him at once.

GONERIL
Pluck out his eyes.

Tear out his eyes.

CORNWALL
Leave him to my displeasure. Edmund, keep you our
sister company: the revenges we are bound to take
upon your traitorous father are not fit for your beholding. Advise the duke, where you are going, to
a most festinate preparation: we are bound to the like. Our posts shall be swift and intelligent betwixt us. Farewell, dear sister: farewell, my lord of Gloucester.

*Leave his punishment to me. Edmund, you keep my sister company: the punishment we are going to have to give
your traitorous father is not fit for you to see. Tell the Duke, to whom you are going, to hurry and get ready for war: we are doing the same. The information will fly quickly between us. Farewell, dear sister: farewell, my lord of Gloucester.*

Enter OSWALD
How now! where's the king?

Hello there! Where's the King?

OSWALD
My lord of Gloucester hath convey'd him hence:
Some five or six and thirty of his knights,
Hot questrists after him, met him at gate;
Who, with some other of the lord's dependants,
Are gone with him towards Dover; where they boast
To have well-armed friends.

*My lord of Gloucester has carried him away: thirty-five or thirty-six of his knights,
who had been urgently seeking him, met him at the gate; they, with some of the other servants of Gloucester,
have gone with him towards Dover; they say they have well armed friends there.*

CORNWALL
Get horses for your mistress.

Get horses for your mistress.

105

GONERIL
Farewell, sweet lord, and sister.

Farewell, sweet lord, and sister.

CORNWALL
Edmund, farewell.

Edmund, farewell.

Exeunt GONERIL, EDMUND, and OSWALD

Go seek the traitor Gloucester,
Pinion him like a thief, bring him before us.

Go and find the traitor Gloucester, tie him like a thief, and bring him to me.

Exeunt other Servants
Though well we may not pass upon his life
Without the form of justice, yet our power
Shall do a courtesy to our wrath, which men
May blame, but not control. Who's there? the traitor?

Though we should not execute him without a fair trial, my position will give way to my anger, which men may blame, but not control. Who's there? The traitor?

Enter GLOUCESTER, brought in by two or three

REGAN
Ingrateful fox! 'tis he.

The ungrateful fox! It's him.

CORNWALL
Bind fast his corky arms.

Tie up his withered arms.

GLOUCESTER
What mean your graces? Good my friends, consider
You are my guests: do me no foul play, friends.

What is the meaning of this, your graces? My good friends, remember that you are my guests: do not harm me, friends.

CORNWALL
Bind him, I say.

Tie him up, I said.

Servants bind him

REGAN
Hard, hard. O filthy traitor!

Make those knots tight. You filthy traitor!

GLOUCESTER
Unmerciful lady as you are, I'm none.

You are a merciless lady, but I'm no traitor.

CORNWALL
To this chair bind him. Villain, thou shalt find--

Tie him to this chair. Villain, you will find–

REGAN plucks his beard

GLOUCESTER
By the kind gods, 'tis most ignobly done
To pluck me by the beard.

By the kind gods, it is an undignified thing, to pull at my beard.

REGAN
So white, and such a traitor!

So white, and such a traitor!

GLOUCESTER
Naughty lady,
These hairs, which thou dost ravish from my chin,
Will quicken, and accuse thee: I am your host:
With robbers' hands my hospitable favours
You should not ruffle thus. What will you do?

You bad lady, these hairs, which you pull from my chin, will come to life, and accuse you: I am your host: you should not be so violent to your host's face with your robbing hands. What do you want?

CORNWALL
Come, sir, what letters had you late from France?

Now, sir, what letters did you recently have from France?

REGAN
Be simple answerer, for we know the truth.

Give us a straight answer, because we know the truth.

CORNWALL
And what confederacy have you with the traitors
Late footed in the kingdom?

And what are your links with the traitors who have recently landed in the kingdom?

REGAN
To whose hands have you sent the lunatic king?
Speak.

Where have you sent the lunatic king? Speak.

GLOUCESTER
I have a letter guessingly set down,
Which came from one that's of a neutral heart,
And not from one opposed.

I have a speculative letter, which came from someone who is neutral, not an enemy.

CORNWALL
Cunning.

Cunning.

REGAN
And false.

And a lie.

CORNWALL
Where hast thou sent the king?

Where have you sent the King?

GLOUCESTER
To Dover.

REGAN
Wherefore to Dover? Wast thou not charged at peril--

CORNWALL
Wherefore to Dover? Let him first answer that.

GLOUCESTER
I am tied to the stake, and I must stand the course.

REGAN
Wherefore to Dover, sir?

GLOUCESTER
Because I would not see thy cruel nails
Pluck out his poor old eyes; nor thy fierce sister
In his anointed flesh stick boarish fangs.
The sea, with such a storm as his bare head
In hell-black night endured, would have buoy'd up,
And quench'd the stelled fires:
Yet, poor old heart, he holp the heavens to rain.
If wolves had at thy gate howl'd that stern time,
Thou shouldst have said 'Good porter, turn the key,'
All cruels else subscribed: but I shall see
The winged vengeance overtake such children.

CORNWALL
See't shalt thou never. Fellows, hold the chair.
Upon these eyes of thine I'll set my foot.

GLOUCESTER
He that will think to live till he be old,
Give me some help! O cruel! O you gods!

REGAN
One side will mock another; the other too.

CORNWALL
If you see vengeance,--

To Dover.

Why to Dover? Were you not ordered on pain of death—

Why to Dover? Let him answer that first.

I am at their mercy, I must be strong.

Why to Dover, sir?

Because I did not want to see your cruel nails tear out his poor old eyes; nor see your fierce sister stick her boar's fangs into his God-appointed flesh. If the sea had to face such a storm as he did with his bare head in the hell black night, it would have risen up and put out the light of the stars: yet, poor old heart, he called on the heavens to rain. If wolves had howled at your gates at that terrible time, you should have said, "good Porter, let them in." Forget all your other cruel deeds, but I shall see that vengeance will overtake you for your treatment of your father.

You never will see it. You men, hold the chair. I shall kick your eyes out.

Anyone who wants a long life, help me! Oh cruelty! Oh you gods!

One side can mock the other; the other will give it back.

If you see vengeance—

First Servant
Hold your hand, my lord:
I have served you ever since I was a child;
But better service have I never done you
Than now to bid you hold.

Hold back, my lord:
I have served you ever since I was a child;
but I have never served you so well
as I do now in telling you to stop.

REGAN
How now, you dog!

What's this, you dog!

First Servant
If you did wear a beard upon your chin,
I'd shake it on this quarrel.

If you had a beard on your chin,
I'd pull it in this argument.

REGAN
What do you mean?

What do you mean?

CORNWALL
My villain!

This is my villain!

They draw and fight

First Servant
Nay, then, come on, and take the chance of anger.

Bring it on then, and risk fighting when angry.

REGAN
Give me thy sword. A peasant stand up thus!

Give me your sword. How dare a peasant oppose us like this!

Takes a sword, and runs at him behind

First Servant
O, I am slain! My lord, you have one eye left
To see some mischief on him. O!

Oh, you've killed me! My lord, you have one eye left to take revenge. Oh!

Dies

CORNWALL
Lest it see more, prevent it. Out, vile jelly!
Where is thy lustre now?

In case it sees more, we'll stop it. Out with the vile jelly! Where's your sparkle now?

GLOUCESTER
All dark and comfortless. Where's my son Edmund?
Edmund, enkindle all the sparks of nature,
To quit this horrid act.

All is dark and cold. Where's my son Edmund?
Edmund, summon up all your strength,
to take revenge for this.

REGAN
Out, treacherous villain!
Thou call'st on him that hates thee: it was he
That made the overture of thy treasons to us;
Who is too good to pity thee.

Forget it, treacherous villain!
You are calling on someone who hates you: it was him who alerted us to your treason; he is too loyal to pity you.

GLOUCESTER
O my follies! then Edgar was abused.
Kind gods, forgive me that, and prosper him!

How stupid I have been! So Edgar was wronged. Kind gods, forgive me for that, and help him to prosper!

REGAN
Go thrust him out at gates, and let him smell
His way to Dover.

Throw him out of doors, and let him smell his way to Dover.

Exit one with GLOUCESTER
How is't, my lord? how look you?

How goes it, my lord? How are you?

CORNWALL
I have received a hurt: follow me, lady.
Turn out that eyeless villain; throw this slave
Upon the dunghill. Regan, I bleed apace:
Untimely comes this hurt: give me your arm.

I have been wounded: follow me, lady. Throw out that blind villain; throw this slave on the dungheap. Regan, I'm bleeding badly: this is a bad time to be wounded: give me your arm.

Exit CORNWALL, led by REGAN

Second Servant
I'll never care what wickedness I do,
If this man come to good.

I'll never care about doing wicked things, if this man comes to judgement.

Third Servant
If she live long,
And in the end meet the old course of death,
Women will all turn monsters.

If a woman lives long enough, and finds a natural death, she will always become a monster.

Second Servant
Let's follow the old earl, and get the Bedlam
To lead him where he would: his roguish madness
Allows itself to any thing.

Let's follow the old earl, and let the madman lead him where he wants: his strange madness permits him to do anything.

Third Servant
Go thou: I'll fetch some flax and whites of eggs
To apply to his bleeding face. Now, heaven help him!

You go: I'll get some flax and egg whites to treat his bleeding face. Now, may heaven help him!

110

Exeunt severally

Act 4

SCENE I. The heath.

Enter EDGAR

EDGAR
Yet better thus, and known to be contemn'd,
Than still contemn'd and flatter'd. To be worst,
The lowest and most dejected thing of fortune,
Stands still in esperance, lives not in fear:
The lamentable change is from the best;
The worst returns to laughter. Welcome, then,
Thou unsubstantial air that I embrace!
The wretch that thou hast blown unto the worst
Owes nothing to thy blasts. But who comes here?

It's better to be like this, knowing you are dammed, than to be dammed but think you're not because of flattery. To be the worst, the lowest and most badly treated by Fortune, one can still hope, and does not live in fear: the horrible change is for the best; things can only get better. So welcome you empty air that I embrace: the wretch that you have blown into the worst situation cannot be blown any further. But who's this coming?

Enter GLOUCESTER, led by an Old Man
My father, poorly led? World, world, O world!
But that thy strange mutations make us hate thee,
Life would not yield to age.

My father, led like a beggar? World, world, oh world! Your strange changes make us hate you and make us reconciled to the fact that we shall die.

Old Man
O, my good lord, I have been your tenant, and your father's tenant, these fourscore years.

Oh my good lord, I have been your tenant, and your father's tenant, the past eighty years.

GLOUCESTER
Away, get thee away; good friend, be gone:
Thy comforts can do me no good at all;
Thee they may hurt.

Go away, go away; good friend, go away: you cannot help me and you are putting yourself in danger.

Old Man
Alack, sir, you cannot see your way.

Alas, sir, you cannot see where you're going.

GLOUCESTER
I have no way, and therefore want no eyes;
I stumbled when I saw: full oft 'tis seen,
Our means secure us, and our mere defects
Prove our commodities. O dear son Edgar,
The food of thy abused father's wrath!
Might I but live to see thee in my touch,
I'ld say I had eyes again!

I have nowhere to go, and so I don't need eyes; when I could see I stumbled: it often happens that when things are going well we become complacent, hardship can point us to the truth. Oh my dear son Edgar, the subject of your abused father's anger! If I could live to feel your hand again, it would be as good as having my eyes back!

Old Man
How now! Who's there?

What's that! Who's there?

113

EDGAR
[Aside] O gods! Who is't can say 'I am at the worst'?
I am worse than e'er I was.

Oh gods! Who can say, "I've hit rock bottom"? Now things are worse than ever.

Old Man
'Tis poor mad Tom.

It's poor mad Tom.

EDGAR
[Aside] And worse I may be yet: the worst is not
So long as we can say 'This is the worst.'

And I may be worse still: as long as we can say "this is the worst," we have not reached the bottom.

Old Man
Fellow, where goest?

Where are you going, my man?

GLOUCESTER
Is it a beggar-man?

Is it a beggar?

Old Man
Madman and beggar too.

A beggar and a madman too.

GLOUCESTER
He has some reason, else he could not beg.
I' the last night's storm I such a fellow saw;
Which made me think a man a worm: my son
Came then into my mind; and yet my mind
Was then scarce friends with him: I have heard more since.
As flies to wanton boys, are we to the gods.
They kill us for their sport.

He must have some sense, or he could not beg. I saw a fellow like this in last night's storm; he made me think men are only worms: then I thought of my son; even though my mind at that time hated him: I have heard differently since. The gods treat us like cruel boys treat flies, they kill us for fun.

EDGAR
[Aside] How should this be?
Bad is the trade that must play fool to sorrow,
Angering itself and others.--Bless thee, master!

How has it come to this? It's a bad job when I have to be a fool in the face of all this sorrow, annoying myself and others. Bless you, master!

GLOUCESTER
Is that the naked fellow?

Is that the naked fellow?

Old Man
Ay, my lord.

Yes, my lord.

GLOUCESTER
Then, prithee, get thee gone: if, for my sake,
Thou wilt o'ertake us, hence a mile or twain,

Then, please go: if to help me you should overtake us a mile or two from here on the way

114

I' the way toward Dover, do it for ancient love;
And bring some covering for this naked soul,
Who I'll entreat to lead me.

Old Man
Alack, sir, he is mad.

GLOUCESTER
'Tis the times' plague, when madmen lead the blind.
Do as I bid thee, or rather do thy pleasure;
Above the rest, be gone.

Old Man
I'll bring him the best 'parel that I have,
Come on't what will.

Exit

GLOUCESTER
Sirrah, naked fellow,--

EDGAR
Poor Tom's a-cold.

Aside
I cannot daub it further.

GLOUCESTER
Come hither, fellow.

EDGAR
[Aside] And yet I must.--Bless thy sweet eyes, they bleed.

GLOUCESTER
Know'st thou the way to Dover?

EDGAR
Both stile and gate, horse-way and foot-path. Poor
Tom hath been scared out of his good wits: bless thee, good man's son, from the foul fiend! five fiends have been in poor Tom at once; of lust, as Obidicut; Hobbididence, prince of dumbness; Mahu, of

---

towards Dover, do so for your old loyalty; and bring some clothes for this naked man, whom I'll ask to guide me.

Unfortunately, sir, he is mad.

It's a sign of these bad times, that madmen are leading the blind.
Do as I ask, or rather do what you wish; most importantly, go.

I'll bring him the best clothes that I have, whatever happens.

Sir, you naked chap–

Poor Tom's cold.

I can't keep this up any longer.

Come here, fellow.

But I must.–Bless your sweet eyes, they are bleeding.

Do you know the way to Dover?

I know the way by gates and stiles, bridle path and footpath. Poor Tom has been scared out of his mind: you good man's son, may the gods save you from the devil! Poor Tom has been possessed by five devils at once; the lustful one, Obidicut; Hobbididence, the dumb one; Mahu, the thief;

stealing; Modo, of murder; Flibbertigibbet, of mopping and mowing, who since possesses chambermaids
and waiting-women. So, bless thee, master!

Modo, the murderer; Flibbertigibbet, the puller of faces, who now possesses chambermaids
and serving girls. So, bless you, master!

GLOUCESTER
Here, take this purse, thou whom the heavens' plagues
Have humbled to all strokes: that I am wretched
Makes thee the happier: heavens, deal so still!
Let the superfluous and lust-dieted man,
That slaves your ordinance, that will not see
Because he doth not feel, feel your power quickly;
So distribution should undo excess,
And each man have enough. Dost thou know Dover?

Here, take this purse, you whom the gods have treated so badly
that you accept all misfortunes: my wretchedness
should make you happier: gods, keep it like this!
Let the overfed and greedy man,
who disrespects your position, who is blind through lack of empathy, get some feelings;
that way sharing would remedy greed
and each man would have enough. Do you know Dover?

EDGAR
Ay, master.

Yes, master.

GLOUCESTER
There is a cliff, whose high and bending head
Looks fearfully in the confined deep:
Bring me but to the very brim of it,
And I'll repair the misery thou dost bear
With something rich about me: from that place
I shall no leading need.

There is a cliff whose high overhanging head
looks terrifyingly down into the channeled sea:
just bring me to the very edge of it
and I'll pay you for your pains
with one of my treasures: I shall not need
to be led away from that place.

EDGAR
Give me thy arm:
Poor Tom shall lead thee.

Give me your arm:
Poor Tom will lead you.

Exeunt

SCENE II. Before ALBANY's palace.

Enter GONERIL and EDMUND

GONERIL
Welcome, my lord: I marvel our mild husband
Not met us on the way.

	Welcome, my lord: I'm surprised my sweet husband didn't meet us on the way.

Enter OSWALD
Now, where's your master'?

	Now, where's your master?

OSWALD
Madam, within; but never man so changed.
I told him of the army that was landed;
He smiled at it: I told him you were coming:
His answer was 'The worse:' of Gloucester's treachery,
And of the loyal service of his son,
When I inform'd him, then he call'd me sot,
And told me I had turn'd the wrong side out:
What most he should dislike seems pleasant to him;
What like, offensive.

	Madam, he's inside; I never saw a man so changed. I told him about the army that had landed; he smiled: I told him you were coming: his answer was, "that's bad": I told him about Gloucester's treachery, and how his son served you loyally, when I told him he called me a fool, and told me I had everything back to front: he seems to like the things he should hate, and find the things he should like offensive.

GONERIL
[**To EDMUND**] Then shall you go no further.
It is the cowish terror of his spirit,
That dares not undertake: he'll not feel wrongs
Which tie him to an answer. Our wishes on the way
May prove effects. Back, Edmund, to my brother;
Hasten his musters and conduct his powers:
I must change arms at home, and give the distaff
Into my husband's hands. This trusty servant
Shall pass between us: ere long you are like to hear,
If you dare venture in your own behalf,
A mistress's command. Wear this; spare speech;

	Then you will go no further. This is down to his cowardly spirit, that doesn't dare do anything: he won't be offended by anything if it means he might have to act. Our plans on the way might get him moving. Go back to my brother, Edmund; speed up the gathering of his army and direct his forces: I must change our household positions, and give my husband the apron. This trustworthy servant will be our go-between; before long you are likely to hear, if you dare to do things for yourself, the command of a mistress. Wear this; don't talk;

Giving a favour
Decline your head: this kiss, if it durst speak,
Would stretch thy spirits up into the air:
Conceive, and fare thee well.

	bend down your head: this kiss, if it could talk, would raise your spirits to the heights: believe, and farewell.

117

EDMUND
Yours in the ranks of death.

I'm yours until death.

GONERIL
My most dear Gloucester!

My dearest Gloucester!

Exit EDMUND
O, the difference of man and man!
To thee a woman's services are due:
My fool usurps my bed.

*Oh how different one man is from another!
You deserve a woman's favors:
there's an idiot in my bed.*

OSWALD
Madam, here comes my lord.

Madam, here comes my lord.

Exit

Enter ALBANY

GONERIL
I have been worth the whistle.

Once I was worth coming to meet.

ALBANY
O Goneril!
You are not worth the dust which the rude wind
Blows in your face. I fear your disposition:
That nature, which contemns its origin,
Cannot be border'd certain in itself;
She that herself will sliver and disbranch
From her material sap, perforce must wither
And come to deadly use.

*Oh Goneril!
You are not worth the dust which the rough
wind blows in your face. I fear your character:
the nature of someone who condemns their
parents cannot be thought of as properly
balanced; the one who will cut herself off
from her family tree will surely wither
and eventually die.*

GONERIL
No more; the text is foolish.

That's enough, this is foolish talk.

ALBANY
Wisdom and goodness to the vile seem vile:
Filths savour but themselves. What have you done?
Tigers, not daughters, what have you perform'd?
A father, and a gracious aged man,
Whose reverence even the head-lugg'd bear would lick,
Most barbarous, most degenerate! have you madded.
Could my good brother suffer you to do it?

*To those who are vile, wisdom and goodness
seem vile:
foulness only tastes itself. What have you done?
Wild beasts, not daughters, what have you
done? A father, a good old man—
whom even a trapped bear would show respect
to,
however barbaric and degenerate it was!—you
have driven mad.
How could my good brother have let you do it?*

118

A man, a prince, by him so benefited!
If that the heavens do not their visible spirits
Send quickly down to tame these vile offences,
It will come,
Humanity must perforce prey on itself,
Like monsters of the deep.

GONERIL
Milk-liver'd man!
That bear'st a cheek for blows, a head for wrongs;
Who hast not in thy brows an eye discerning
Thine honour from thy suffering; that not know'st
Fools do those villains pity who are punish'd
Ere they have done their mischief. Where's thy drum?
France spreads his banners in our noiseless land;
With plumed helm thy state begins to threat;
Whiles thou, a moral fool, sit'st still, and criest
'Alack, why does he so?'

ALBANY
See thyself, devil!
Proper deformity seems not in the fiend
So horrid as in woman.

GONERIL
O vain fool!

ALBANY
Thou changed and self-cover'd thing, for shame,
Be-monster not thy feature. Were't my fitness
To let these hands obey my blood,
They are apt enough to dislocate and tear
Thy flesh and bones: howe'er thou art a fiend,
A woman's shape doth shield thee.

GONERIL
Marry, your manhood now--

Enter a Messenger

ALBANY
What news?

*A man, a prince, whom he had treated so well!
If the heavens do not quickly send down their
physical messengers to punish these horrible
crimes, it will turn out
that humankind will turn on itself,
like the monsters of the sea.*

*You lily-livered man!
You have a cheek for slapping, a head to hurt;
you do not have the sense to see the difference
between what should be tolerated and what not;
you don't know
that only fools pity those villains who get punished
in order to prevent their mischief. Where's your drum?
France is raising his flags in our silent land;
in his plumed helmet he is beginning to threaten
your state, while you sit here moralising, and
crying, "Alas, why is he doing this?"*

*Look at yourself, devil!
The deformity which suits a demon
looks more horrible in a woman.*

You stupid fool!

*You changed and disguised thing, for shame,
take that devilish look off your face. If I was
inclined to let my hands obey my feelings
they would be ready to separate and tear
your flesh and your bones: but however evil you
are your woman's body protects you.*

Right, well your manhood–

What is the news?

119

Messenger
O, my good lord, the Duke of Cornwall's dead:
Slain by his servant, going to put out
The other eye of Gloucester.

ALBANY
Gloucester's eye!

Messenger
A servant that he bred, thrill'd with remorse,
Opposed against the act, bending his sword
To his great master; who, thereat enraged,
Flew on him, and amongst them fell'd him dead;
But not without that harmful stroke, which since
Hath pluck'd him after.

ALBANY
This shows you are above,
You justicers, that these our nether crimes
So speedily can venge! But, O poor Gloucester!
Lost he his other eye?

Messenger
Both, both, my lord.
This letter, madam, craves a speedy answer;
'Tis from your sister.

GONERIL
[Aside] One way I like this well;
But being widow, and my Gloucester with her,
May all the building in my fancy pluck
Upon my hateful life: another way,
The news is not so tart.--I'll read, and answer.

Exit

ALBANY
Where was his son when they did take his eyes?

Messenger
Come with my lady hither.

ALBANY
He is not here.

Oh, my good lord, the Duke of Cornwall is dead: killed by his servant as he went to put out Gloucester's other eye.

Gloucester's eye!

A servant whom he had raised, full of remorse, fought against him, drawing his sword against his great master; enraged by this his master attacked him and struck him dead, but not without receiving the fatal wound, which later killed him too.

This shows you are still sitting above, you justices, that can so quickly punish our crimes down below! But oh, poor Gloucester! Did he lose his other eye?

He lost them both, my lord. This letter, madam, begs for a quick reply; it is from your sister.

In one way I'm pleased with this; but now she is a widow, and has my Gloucester with her, she could destroy all my fantasies and ruin my life: in another way the news is not so bad.–I'll read it, and answer.

Where was his son when they blinded him?

Coming here with my lady.

He is not here.

120

Messenger
No, my good lord; I met him back again.

ALBANY
Knows he the wickedness?

Messenger
Ay, my good lord; 'twas he inform'd against him;
And quit the house on purpose, that their punishment
Might have the freer course.

ALBANY
Gloucester, I live
To thank thee for the love thou show'dst the king,
And to revenge thine eyes. Come hither, friend:
Tell me what more thou know'st.

Exeunt

No, my good lord; I met him going back.

Does he know of the wickedness?

Yes, my good lord; it was he who turned him in; he left the house on purpose, so that they could have more freedom to carry out their punishment.

Gloucester, I dedicate my life to thanking you for the love that you showed the King, and to revenge your blinding. Come with me, friend: tell me what else you know.

SCENE III. The French camp near Dover.

Enter KENT and a Gentleman

KENT
Why the King of France is so suddenly gone back
know you the reason?

Do you know why the King of France has so suddenly gone back?

Gentleman
Something he left imperfect in the
state, which since his coming forth is thought
of; which imports to the kingdom so much
fear and danger, that his personal return was
most required and necessary.

He had left something in a bad way in his country which he has thought of since he left; it was a matter of such danger to the kingdom that it was essential for him to return and deal with it personally.

KENT
Who hath he left behind him general?

Who has he left behind in charge?

Gentleman
The Marshal of France, Monsieur La Far.

The Marshal of France, Monsieur La Far.

KENT
Did your letters pierce the queen to any demonstration of grief?

Did your letters seem to cause the Queen any unhappiness?

Gentleman
Ay, sir; she took them, read them in my presence;
And now and then an ample tear trill'd down
Her delicate cheek: it seem'd she was a queen
Over her passion; who, most rebel-like,
Sought to be king o'er her.

Yes, sir; she took them and read them in my presence; now and then a great tear would roll down her delicate cheek: it seemed that she was controlling her feelings, which threatened to overcome her.

KENT
O, then it moved her.

Oh, so it moved her.

Gentleman
Not to a rage: patience and sorrow strove
Who should express her goodliest. You have seen
Sunshine and rain at once: her smiles and tears
Were like a better way: those happy smilets,
That play'd on her ripe lip, seem'd not to know
What guests were in her eyes; which parted

Not to anger: self-control and sadness fought to give her the most beautiful expression. You have seen sunshine and rain at the same time: her smiles and tears were similar, but better: those little smiles which played on her ripe lips seemed to be unaware of the tears in her eyes, which fell

122

thence,
As pearls from diamonds dropp'd. In brief,
Sorrow would be a rarity most beloved,
If all could so become it.

KENT
Made she no verbal question?

Gentleman
'Faith, once or twice she heaved the name of 'father'
Pantingly forth, as if it press'd her heart:
Cried 'Sisters! sisters! Shame of ladies! sisters!
Kent! father! sisters! What, i' the storm? i' the night?
Let pity not be believed!' There she shook
The holy water from her heavenly eyes,
And clamour moisten'd: then away she started
To deal with grief alone.

KENT
It is the stars,
The stars above us, govern our conditions;
Else one self mate and make could not beget
Such different issues. You spoke not with her since?

Gentleman
No.

KENT
Was this before the king return'd?

Gentleman
No, since.

KENT
Well, sir, the poor distressed Lear's i' the town;
Who sometime, in his better tune, remembers
What we are come about, and by no means
Will yield to see his daughter.

Gentleman
Why, good sir?

KENT

*from there
like pearls dropping from diamonds. To sum up,
everyone would love sorrow
if everybody showed it like this.*

Did she ask no questions?

*Well once or twice she sighed the name 'father'
as if it was breaking her heart:
she cried out, 'Sisters! Sisters! You're a shame
to womankind! Sisters!
Kent! Father! Sisters! What, in the storm? In the night?
For pity's sake let this be untrue!' Then she
burst out with holy tears from her wonderful
eyes, and her words were lost in her sobs: then
she went away to deal with her grief in private.*

*It is the stars,
the stars above us, which control our nature;
otherwise two people could not breed
such different children. You haven't spoken to
her since?*

No.

Was this before the king returned?

No, since.

*Well, sir, poor distressed Lear is in the town;
who occasionally, when he's in his senses,
remembers why we have come, and refuses
to see his daughter.*

Why, good sir?

123

A sovereign shame so elbows him: his own unkindness,
That stripp'd her from his benediction, turn'd her
To foreign casualties, gave her dear rights
To his dog-hearted daughters, these things sting
His mind so venomously, that burning shame
Detains him from Cordelia.

Gentleman
Alack, poor gentleman!

KENT
Of Albany's and Cornwall's powers you heard not?

Gentleman
'Tis so, they are afoot.

KENT
Well, sir, I'll bring you to our master Lear,
And leave you to attend him: some dear cause
Will in concealment wrap me up awhile;
When I am known aright, you shall not grieve
Lending me this acquaintance. I pray you, go
Along with me.

Exeunt

He is overcome with shame: his own unkindness, that stripped her of his blessing, made her take her chances abroad, gave her proper inheritance to his dog hearted daughters, these things prick his conscience so badly that a burning shame keeps him from Cordelia.

Alas, poor gentleman!

Did you hear anything about Albany and Cornwall's armies?

Yes, they are on the march.

Well, sir, I will take you to our master Lear, and leave you to look after him: I have an important purpose which means I must remain disguised for a while; when my identity is revealed, you will not regret your friendship to me. Please, come along with me.

SCENE IV. The same. A tent.

Enter, with drum and colours, CORDELIA, Doctor, and Soldiers

CORDELIA
Alack, 'tis he: why, he was met even now
As mad as the vex'd sea; singing aloud;
Crown'd with rank fumiter and furrow-weeds,
With bur-docks, hemlock, nettles, cuckoo-flowers,
Darnel, and all the idle weeds that grow
In our sustaining corn. A century send forth;
Search every acre in the high-grown field,
And bring him to our eye.

Alas, it is him: why, he has been seen just now raging like the sea; singing aloud; wearing a crown of stinking plants and weeds, with burdock, hemlock, nettles, cowslip, rye, and all the useless weeds that grow in the useful corn. Send out a platoon; search every acre of the tall cornfields and bring him to see me.

Exit an Officer
What can man's wisdom
In the restoring his bereaved sense?
He that helps him take all my outward worth.

What science is there that can bring him back to his senses? Anyone who can help can have all my possessions.

Doctor
There is means, madam:
Our foster-nurse of nature is repose,
The which he lacks; that to provoke in him,
Are many simples operative, whose power
Will close the eye of anguish.

There is a way, madam: the great healer of nature is rest, which he is lacking; to give him that there are many herbs, whose power will ease his pain.

CORDELIA
All blest secrets,
All you unpublish'd virtues of the earth,
Spring with my tears! be aidant and remediate
In the good man's distress! Seek, seek for him;
Lest his ungovern'd rage dissolve the life
That wants the means to lead it.

May all the blessed secrets, all the unknown powers of the earth, grow up, watered with my tears! Be healing for this good man's illness! Look, look for him; in case his wild frenzy takes away the life that doesn't have the sanity to look after it.

Enter a Messenger

Messenger
News, madam;
The British powers are marching hitherward.

I have news, madam; the British powers are marching this way.

CORDELIA
'Tis known before; our preparation stands
In expectation of them. O dear father,
It is thy business that I go about;

I knew that already; our forces are ready for them. Oh dear father, I am doing this on your behalf;

Therefore great France
My mourning and important tears hath pitied.
No blown ambition doth our arms incite,
But love, dear love, and our aged father's right:
Soon may I hear and see him!

Exeunt

*that is why great France
took pity on my sorrow and begging tears.
No arrogant ambition drives me on,
but love, dear love and my aged father's rights:
I hope I may soon hear and see him!*

SCENE V. Gloucester's castle.

Enter REGAN and OSWALD

REGAN
But are my brother's powers set forth?

But have my brother's forces set out?

OSWALD
Ay, madam.

Yes madam.

REGAN
Himself in person there?

And is he there in person?

OSWALD
Madam, with much ado:
Your sister is the better soldier.

*Yes madam, after a great fuss:
your sister is the better soldier.*

REGAN
Lord Edmund spake not with your lord at home?

Did Lord Edmund not speak to your lord at home?

OSWALD
No, madam.

No, madam.

REGAN
What might import my sister's letter to him?

What was the meaning of my sister's letter to him?

OSWALD
I know not, lady.

I do not know, lady.

REGAN
'Faith, he is posted hence on serious matter.
It was great ignorance, Gloucester's eyes being out,
To let him live: where he arrives he moves
All hearts against us: Edmund, I think, is gone,
In pity of his misery, to dispatch
His nighted life: moreover, to descry
The strength o' the enemy.

*By God, he is coming here on serious business.
It was very stupid to let Gloucester live
after blinding him: wherever he goes he turns
everyone's hearts against us: Edmund, I think,
has gone to do him the kindness of ending
his blind life: and also to spy out
the enemy's strength.*

OSWALD
I must needs after him, madam, with my letter.

I must follow him, madam, with my letter.

REGAN
Our troops set forth to-morrow: stay with us;
The ways are dangerous.

Our troops are setting out tomorrow: stay with me; the roads are dangerous.

OSWALD
I may not, madam:
My lady charged my duty in this business.

I can't, madam:
my lady ordered me to do this.

REGAN
Why should she write to Edmund? Might not you
Transport her purposes by word? Belike,
Something--I know not what: I'll love thee much,
Let me unseal the letter.

Why would she write to Edmund? Couldn't you just take a verbal message? I think, something–I don't know what: I'll be very pleased with you,
let me read the letter.

OSWALD
Madam, I had rather--

Madam, I would rather–

REGAN
I know your lady does not love her husband;
I am sure of that: and at her late being here
She gave strange oeillades and most speaking looks
To noble Edmund. I know you are of her bosom.

I know your lady does not love her husband; I'm sure of that: and when she was here recently she was giving meaningful winks and amorous glances
to noble Edmund. I know you are in her confidence.

OSWALD
I, madam?

I, madam?

REGAN
I speak in understanding; you are; I know't:
Therefore I do advise you, take this note:
My lord is dead; Edmund and I have talk'd;
And more convenient is he for my hand
Than for your lady's: you may gather more.
If you do find him, pray you, give him this;
And when your mistress hears thus much from you,
I pray, desire her call her wisdom to her.
So, fare you well.
If you do chance to hear of that blind traitor,
Preferment falls on him that cuts him off.

I know what I'm talking about; you are, I know it:
so I advise you to think about this:
my Lord is dead; Edmund and I have talked;
and he prefers my hand to that
of your lady's: you may find out more.
If you do find him, please give him this;
and when your mistress hears of this from you,
please ask to come to her senses.
So, farewell.
If you do happen to find that blind traitor,
there will be promotion for the one who kills him.

OSWALD
Would I could meet him, madam! I should show
What party I do follow.

I wish I could meet him, madam! Then I would show
where my loyalties lie.

REGAN
Fare thee well.

Farewell.

128

Exeunt

SCENE VI. Fields near Dover.

Enter GLOUCESTER, and EDGAR dressed like a peasant

GLOUCESTER
When shall we come to the top of that same hill? | *When will we get to the top of the hill we want?*

EDGAR
You do climb up it now: look, how we labour. | *You are climbing up it now: look what hard work it is.*

GLOUCESTER
Methinks the ground is even. | *I think the ground is flat.*

EDGAR
Horrible steep. | *It's terribly steep.*
Hark, do you hear the sea? | *Listen, can you hear the sea?*

GLOUCESTER
No, truly. | *Definitely not.*

EDGAR
Why, then, your other senses grow imperfect | *Well, your other senses must've been damaged*
By your eyes' anguish. | *by the pain in your eyes.*

GLOUCESTER
So may it be, indeed: | *That may well be the case:*
Methinks thy voice is alter'd; and thou speak'st | *I think your voice has changed, you speak*
In better phrase and matter than thou didst. | *more sense, and more articulately, and you did.*

EDGAR
You're much deceived: in nothing am I changed | *You're much mistaken: I have changed nothing*
But in my garments. | *but my clothes.*

GLOUCESTER
Methinks you're better spoken. | *I think you're better spoken.*

EDGAR
Come on, sir; here's the place: stand still. How fearful | *Come on, sir; here's the place: stand still. How terrifying*
And dizzy 'tis, to cast one's eyes so low! | *and dizzying it is, to look down so far!*
The crows and choughs that wing the midway air | *The crows and jackdaws that fly through the air in between*
Show scarce so gross as beetles: half way down | *hardly look as big as beetles: halfway down*
Hangs one that gathers samphire, dreadful trade! | *one of the samphire gatherers is hanging, what*
Methinks he seems no bigger than his head: | *a dreadful job! I think he looks no bigger than*

130

The fishermen, that walk upon the beach, / Appear like mice; and yond tall anchoring bark, / Diminish'd to her cock; her cock, a buoy / Almost too small for sight: the murmuring surge, / That on the unnumber'd idle pebbles chafes, / Cannot be heard so high. I'll look no more; / Lest my brain turn, and the deficient sight / Topple down headlong.	*his head: the fishermen walking on the beach look like mice; that great ship at anchor has shrunk to the size of a rowing boat, her rowing boat looks like a buoy almost too small to be seen: the rumble of the waves that crash on the numberless barren pebbles cannot be heard up here. I won't look any more, in case it makes me dizzy and my sight fails, making me fall headfirst.*
GLOUCESTER / Set me where you stand.	*Put me where you are standing.*
EDGAR / Give me your hand: you are now within a foot / Of the extreme verge: for all beneath the moon / Would I not leap upright.	*Give me your hand: you are now within a foot of the edge: I wouldn't stand up here for everything on earth.*
GLOUCESTER / Let go my hand. / Here, friend, 's another purse; in it a jewel / Well worth a poor man's taking: fairies and gods / Prosper it with thee! Go thou farther off; / Bid me farewell, and let me hear thee going.	*Let go of my hand. Here, friend, is another purse; there's a jewel in it that's well worth having for a poor man: may the fairies and gods make it profitable for you! Go further away; say goodbye, and let me hear you going.*
EDGAR / Now fare you well, good sir.	*Now take care of yourself, good sir.*
GLOUCESTER / With all my heart.	*I fully intend to.*
EDGAR / Why I do trifle thus with his despair / Is done to cure it.	*I am only messing about with his despair so that it can be cured.*
GLOUCESTER / [Kneeling] O you mighty gods! / This world I do renounce, and, in your sights, / Shake patiently my great affliction off: / If I could bear it longer, and not fall / To quarrel with your great opposeless wills, / My snuff and loathed part of nature should / Burn itself out. If Edgar live, O, bless him! / Now, fellow, fare thee well.	*Oh you mighty gods! I am giving up the world, and in your sight I am throwing off my great affliction: if I could bear it any longer, without rebelling against your almighty orders, the almost consumed wick of my candle of life would burn itself out. If Edgar is alive, bless him! Now, my friend, goodbye.*

He falls forward

EDGAR
Gone, sir: farewell.
And yet I know not how conceit may rob
The treasury of life, when life itself
Yields to the theft: had he been where he thought,
By this, had thought been past. Alive or dead?
Ho, you sir! friend! Hear you, sir! speak!
Thus might he pass indeed: yet he revives.
What are you, sir?

I am gone sir, goodbye.
And yet I don't know whether imagination can steal away life, when life gives in to its theft: might he die just because he thinks he has? Is he alive or dead?
Hey, you sir! Friend! Listen, sir! Speak!
He might actually be dead: but he's coming round. How are you sir?

GLOUCESTER
Away, and let me die.

Go away, and let me die.

EDGAR
Hadst thou been aught but gossamer, feathers, air,
So many fathom down precipitating,
Thou'dst shiver'd like an egg: but thou dost breathe;
Hast heavy substance; bleed'st not; speak'st; art sound.
Ten masts at each make not the altitude
Which thou hast perpendicularly fell:
Thy life's a miracle. Speak yet again.

If you had been nothing but gossamer, feathers and air,
falling down so many fathoms you would have smashed like an egg: but you breathe;
you are all in one piece; you don't bleed; you speak; you're all right.
Ten masts one on top of the other would not reach the height which you have just fallen straight down: it's a miracle you're alive. Speak again.

GLOUCESTER
But have I fall'n, or no?

But have I fallen or not?

EDGAR
From the dread summit of this chalky bourn.
Look up a-height; the shrill-gorged lark so far
Cannot be seen or heard: do but look up.

From the terrible top of this chalky cliff.
Look up there; the high singing lark cannot be seen or heard up there: just look up.

GLOUCESTER
Alack, I have no eyes.
Is wretchedness deprived that benefit,
To end itself by death? 'Twas yet some comfort,
When misery could beguile the tyrant's rage,
And frustrate his proud will.

Alas, I am blind.
Is misery deprived of the benefit of ending itself in suicide? It used to be a comfort, when misery could outwit the tyrant's anger and stop him doing what he wanted.

EDGAR
Give me your arm:
Up: so. How is 't? Feel you your legs? You stand.

Give me your arm:
get up: that's it. How is it? Can you feel your legs? Stand up.

GLOUCESTER
Too well, too well.

I can do it all too well.

EDGAR
This is above all strangeness.
Upon the crown o' the cliff, what thing was that
Which parted from you?

*This is beyond belief.
When you were at the top of the cliff, who was
that who left you?*

GLOUCESTER
A poor unfortunate beggar.

A poor unfortunate beggar.

EDGAR
As I stood here below, methought his eyes
Were two full moons; he had a thousand noses,
Horns whelk'd and waved like the enridged sea:
It was some fiend; therefore, thou happy father,
Think that the clearest gods, who make them honours
Of men's impossibilities, have preserved thee.

*As I stood down here, I thought his eyes
were two full moons; he had a thousand noses,
horns twisted and waved like the ridges of the
sea: it was some devil; therefore, you happy
father, consider that the purest gods, who win
our worship through doing impossible things,
have saved you.*

GLOUCESTER
I do remember now: henceforth I'll bear
Affliction till it do cry out itself
'Enough, enough,' and die. That thing you speak of,
I took it for a man; often 'twould say
'The fiend, the fiend:' he led me to that place.

*Now I remember: from now on I'll put up
with my hardships until they cry out themselves
'Enough, enough,' and die. That thing you speak of,
I thought it was a man; often it would say
'The fiend, the fiend:' he took me to that place.*

EDGAR
Bear free and patient thoughts. But who comes here?

Keep your thoughts happy and patient. But who is this?

Enter KING LEAR, fantastically dressed with wild flowers

The safer sense will ne'er accommodate
His master thus.

Keep your thoughts happy and patient. But who is this?

KING LEAR
No, they cannot touch me for coining; I am the king himself.

No, they can't arrest me for forging coins; I am the King himself.

EDGAR
O thou side-piercing sight!

What a heartrending sight!

KING LEAR
Nature's above art in that respect. There's your

Nature's better than art in that respect. Here's

133

press-money. That fellow handles his bow like a crow-keeper: draw me a clothier's yard. Look, look, a mouse! Peace, peace; this piece of toasted
cheese will do 't. There's my gauntlet; I'll prove it on a giant. Bring up the brown bills. O, well flown, bird! i' the clout, i' the clout: hewgh! Give the word.

EDGAR
Sweet marjoram.

KING LEAR
Pass.

GLOUCESTER
I know that voice.

KING LEAR
Ha! Goneril, with a white beard! They flattered me like a dog; and told me I had white hairs in my
beard ere the black ones were there. To say 'ay' and 'no' to every thing that I said!--'Ay' and 'no' too was no good divinity. When the rain came to wet me once, and the wind to make me chatter; when
the thunder would not peace at my bidding; there I
found 'em, there I smelt 'em out. Go to, they are not men o' their words: they told me I was every thing; 'tis a lie, I am not ague-proof.

GLOUCESTER
The trick of that voice I do well remember:
Is 't not the king?

KING LEAR
Ay, every inch a king:
When I do stare, see how the subject quakes.
I pardon that man's life. What was thy cause?
Adultery?
Thou shalt not die: die for adultery! No:
The wren goes to 't, and the small gilded fly
Does lecher in my sight.

---

your signing on money. That fellow handles his bow like a scarecrow: pull the string back as far as it will go. Look, look, a mouse! Hush, hush; this piece of toasted cheese will do it. There's my challenge; I'll take on a giant. Bring up the spearmen. Oh, good shot! It's a bull's-eye, it's a bull's-eye: twang!
What's the password?

Sweet marjoram.

You can pass.

I know that voice.

Ha! Goneril, with a white beard! They flattered me like a dog does its master; they told me I was old and wise
before I was either. They said yes and no to everything I said! Saying yes and no to everything is poor theology. When the rain came to soak me, and the wind to freeze me; when
the thunder would not stop when I told it to; then I
saw what they're like, then I found them out. Go away, they are not men of their word: they told me that I was
everything; that's a lie, I am not fever proof.

That way of speaking is very familiar:
isn't it the King?

Yes, every inch a King:
when I look, see how the subject shakes.
I pardon that man. What was your offence?
Adultery?
You will not die; die for adultery! No:
wrens do it, and little golden flies
do it in my sight.

Let copulation thrive; for Gloucester's bastard son
Was kinder to his father than my daughters
Got 'tween the lawful sheets.
To 't, luxury, pell-mell! for I lack soldiers.
Behold yond simpering dame,
Whose face between her forks presages snow;
That minces virtue, and does shake the head
To hear of pleasure's name;
The fitchew, nor the soiled horse, goes to 't
With a more riotous appetite.
Down from the waist they are Centaurs,
Though women all above:
But to the girdle do the gods inherit,
Beneath is all the fiends';
There's hell, there's darkness, there's the sulphurous pit,
Burning, scalding, stench, consumption; fie, fie, fie! pah, pah! Give me an ounce of civet, good apothecary, to sweeten my imagination: there's money for thee.

GLOUCESTER
O, let me kiss that hand!

KING LEAR
Let me wipe it first; it smells of mortality.

GLOUCESTER
O ruin'd piece of nature! This great world
Shall so wear out to nought. Dost thou know me?

KING LEAR
I remember thine eyes well enough. Dost thou squiny
at me? No, do thy worst, blind Cupid! I'll not love. Read thou this challenge; mark but the penning of it.

GLOUCESTER
Were all the letters suns, I could not see one.

EDGAR
I would not take this from report; it is,
And my heart breaks at it.

Let sex flourish; Gloucester's bastard son was kinder to his father than my daughters who were conceived in marriage. Go to it, lust, willy-nilly!
I lack soldiers. Look at that simpering woman, whose face looks as if she is frigidly chaste; she imitates virtue, and shakes her head at the sound of pleasure;
neither the polecat nor the lusty stallion goes at it with greater enthusiasm.
From the waist down they are centaurs, although they are all women above: the top half belongs to the gods, below it's all the devil's: there's hell, there's darkness,
there is a reeking pit – burning, scalding, stinking, swallowing; fie, fie, fie! pah, pah! Give me an ounce of perfume, good chemist, to sweeten my imagination. There's money for you.

Oh let me kiss that hand!

Let me wipe it first; it smells of death.

What a ruined piece of nature! This great universe will eventually be reduced to nothing like this. Do you know me?

I remember your eyes well enough. Are you squinting at me? Do your worst, blind Cupid! I won't love. Read this challenge; look at the penmanship.

If all the letters were suns, I wouldn't see a single one.

You don't just have to believe the words; it's true, and it breaks my heart.

135

KING LEAR
Read.

GLOUCESTER
What, with the case of eyes?

KING LEAR
O, ho, are you there with me? No eyes in your head, nor no money in your purse? Your eyes are in
a heavy case, your purse in a light; yet you see how
this world goes.

GLOUCESTER
I see it feelingly.

KING LEAR
What, art mad? A man may see how this world goes
with no eyes. Look with thine ears: see how yond
justice rails upon yond simple thief. Hark, in thine ear: change places; and, handy-dandy, which
is the justice, which is the thief? Thou hast seen a farmer's dog bark at a beggar?

GLOUCESTER
Ay, sir.

KING LEAR
And the creature run from the cur? There thou mightst behold the great image of authority: a dog's obeyed in office.
Thou rascal beadle, hold thy bloody hand!
Why dost thou lash that whore? Strip thine own back;
Thou hotly lust'st to use her in that kind
For which thou whipp'st her. The usurer hangs the cozener.
Through tatter'd clothes small vices do appear;
Robes and furr'd gowns hide all. Plate sin with gold,
And the strong lance of justice hurtless breaks:

Read.

What, with my eye sockets?

*Aha, is that what you mean? You have no eyes in your
head, and no money in your purse? Your eyes are too
dark, your purse is too light; but that's the way the world turns.*

I can certainly see that.

*What, are you mad? A man can see how the world turns
without eyes. Look with your ears: see how that judge attacks that lowly thief. Listen with your ears: swap places, take your pick, who is the judge and who is the thief? Have you ever seen
a farmer's dog bark at a beggar?*

Yes, sir.

*And seen the man run from the dog? There you can see a great symbol of authority: a
dog's obeyed when he holds office.
You rascally policeman, hold back your bloody hand! Why do you whip that whore? Whip your own back;
you are dying to do the same thing with her that you're whipping her for. The moneylender hangs the pawnbroker.
Little vices show through tattered clothes; robes and fur lined gowns cover up everything.
Cover sin with gold,
and the strong spear of justice breaks off*

136

Arm it in rags, a pigmy's straw does pierce it.
None does offend, none, I say, none; I'll able 'em:
Take that of me, my friend, who have the power
To seal the accuser's lips. Get thee glass eyes;
And like a scurvy politician, seem
To see the things thou dost not. Now, now, now, now:
Pull off my boots: harder, harder: so.

harmlessly; dress it in rags, and a pigmy's straw can run through it. Nobody has sinned, I say, nobody; I'll vouch for them: take that from me, my friend, who has the power to silence the accuser. Get yourself glass eyes; like a vile trickster, pretend to see the things that you can't. Now, now, now, now; pull off my boots; harder, harder; that's it.

EDGAR
O, matter and impertinency mix'd! Reason in madness!

Oh, sense and irrelevance mixed! Reason in lunacy!

KING LEAR
If thou wilt weep my fortunes, take my eyes.
I know thee well enough; thy name is Gloucester:
Thou must be patient; we came crying hither:
Thou know'st, the first time that we smell the air,
We wawl and cry. I will preach to thee: mark.

If you will cry for my misfortune, take my eyes. I know you well enough; your name is Gloucester: you must be patient; we began our lives crying: you know that from our very first breath we scream and cry. I will preach to you, listen.

GLOUCESTER
Alack, alack the day!

Alas, alas for this time!

KING LEAR
When we are born, we cry that we are come
To this great stage of fools: this a good block;
It were a delicate stratagem, to shoe
A troop of horse with felt: I'll put 't in proof;
And when I have stol'n upon these sons-in-law,
Then, kill, kill, kill, kill, kill, kill!

When we are born, we cry that we have arrived on this great stage of fools: it's a good scaffold; it would be a cunning plan to put felt shoes on the platoon of cavalry: I'll try it; and when I have crept up upon my sons-in-law, then, kill, kill, kill, kill, kill, kill!

Enter a Gentleman, with Attendants

Gentleman
O, here he is: lay hand upon him. Sir,
Your most dear daughter--

Aha, he is: take hold of him. Sir, your dearest daughter–

KING LEAR
No rescue? What, a prisoner? I am even
The natural fool of fortune. Use me well;
You shall have ransom. Let me have surgeons;
I am cut to the brains.

No escape? What, I'm a prisoner? I'm always the toy of fate. Treat me well; you will get a ransom. Let me have surgeons; my brains are damaged.

137

Gentleman
You shall have any thing.

KING LEAR
No seconds? all myself?
Why, this would make a man a man of salt,
To use his eyes for garden water-pots,
Ay, and laying autumn's dust.

Gentleman
Good sir,--

KING LEAR
I will die bravely, like a bridegroom. What!
I will be jovial: come, come; I am a king,
My masters, know you that.

Gentleman
You are a royal one, and we obey you.

KING LEAR
Then there's life in't. Nay, if you get it, you shall get it with running. Sa, sa, sa, sa.

Exit running; Attendants follow

Gentleman
A sight most pitiful in the meanest wretch,
Past speaking of in a king! Thou hast one daughter,
Who redeems nature from the general curse
Which twain have brought her to.

EDGAR
Hail, gentle sir.

Gentleman
Sir, speed you: what's your will?

EDGAR
Do you hear aught, sir, of a battle toward?

Gentleman
Most sure and vulgar: every one hears that,
Which can distinguish sound.

You shall have anything you want.

*No backers? I'm all alone?
Why, this could turn a man to tears,
he could use his eyes to water his garden
and settle the dust in the autumn.*

Good sir—

*I will make a good show of my death, like a bridegroom. What!
I will be jolly: come along; I am a king,
my masters, you should know that.*

You are royal, and we obey you.

*Then there's still hope. No, if you want it
you'll have to catch it. Tally Ho!*

*This would be an awful sight if he was the lowest wretch,
it's beyond imagining in a King! You have one daughter,
who saves your blood from the general curse
the other two have brought upon it.*

Greetings, good sir.

The same to you sir: what do you want?

Do you hear any talk, sir, of a battle coming?

Certainly, it's common knowledge: everyone's heard of it who has ears to listen.

EDGAR
But, by your favour,
How near's the other army?

But, if you don't mind,
how close is the other army?

Gentleman
Near and on speedy foot; the main descry
Stands on the hourly thought.

They are near and moving fast; they are
expected to be spotted any hour now.

EDGAR
I thank you, sir: that's all.

Thank you, sir: that's all.

Gentleman
Though that the queen on special cause is here,
Her army is moved on.

Although the Queen has stayed here for a
special reason her army has moved on.

EDGAR
I thank you, sir.

Thank you, sir.

Exit Gentleman

GLOUCESTER
You ever-gentle gods, take my breath from me:
Let not my worser spirit tempt me again
To die before you please!

You eternally kind gods, take my breath away:
don't let my dark side tempt me again
to die before you wish!

EDGAR
Well pray you, father.

That's a good prayer, father.

GLOUCESTER
Now, good sir, what are you?

Now, good sir, who are you?

EDGAR
A most poor man, made tame to fortune's blows;
Who, by the art of known and feeling sorrows,
Am pregnant to good pity. Give me your hand,
I'll lead you to some biding.

A very poor man, accustomed to the blows of
fate, who, being used to feeling sorrow,
is very ready to give pity. Give me your hand,
I'll lead you to some lodging.

GLOUCESTER
Hearty thanks:
The bounty and the benison of heaven
To boot, and boot!

My hearty thanks:
may you have the rewards and blessings of
heaven
in addition, and more!

Enter OSWALD

OSWALD
A proclaim'd prize! Most happy!

Here's the advertised prize! What a piece of

That eyeless head of thine was first framed flesh
To raise my fortunes. Thou old unhappy traitor,
Briefly thyself remember: the sword is out
That must destroy thee.

GLOUCESTER
Now let thy friendly hand
Put strength enough to't.

EDGAR interposes

OSWALD
Wherefore, bold peasant,
Darest thou support a publish'd traitor? Hence;
Lest that the infection of his fortune take
Like hold on thee. Let go his arm.

EDGAR
Ch'ill not let go, zir, without vurther 'casion.

OSWALD
Let go, slave, or thou diest!

EDGAR
Good gentleman, go your gait, and let poor volk
pass. An chud ha' bin zwaggered out of my life,
'twould not ha' bin zo long as 'tis by a vortnight.
Nay, come not near th' old man; keep out, che vor
ye, or ise try whether your costard or my ballow be
the harder: ch'ill be plain with you.

OSWALD
Out, dunghill!

EDGAR
Ch'ill pick your teeth, zir: come; no matter vor
your foins.

They fight, and EDGAR knocks him down

OSWALD
Slave, thou hast slain me: villain, take my purse:

---

luck! That blind head of yours was created
to lift my fortunes. You unhappy old traitor,
make your peace with heaven: the sword is
drawn which will kill you.

May your friendly hand
have the strength to do it.

By what right, cheeky peasant,
do you dare to support a known traitor? Get
lost,
in case you catch the infection of his bad luck
and get the same treatment. Let go of his arm.

I won't let go, sir, without being given a reason.

Let go, slave, or you're dead!

Good gentleman, go about your business, and
let poor folk
pass. If I could be bullied out of my life,
I would have been dead a fortnight ago.
No, don't come near the old man; keep off, I
warn
you, or we'll see whether your apple or my stick
is the harder: I'm being straight with you.

Get away, dunghill!

I'll pick your teeth, sir: bring it on; I'm not
scared
of your thrusts.

Slave, you have killed me: villain, take my

If ever thou wilt thrive, bury my body;
And give the letters which thou find'st about me
To Edmund earl of Gloucester; seek him out
Upon the British party: O, untimely death!

Dies

EDGAR
I know thee well: a serviceable villain;
As duteous to the vices of thy mistress
As badness would desire.

GLOUCESTER
What, is he dead?

EDGAR
Sit you down, father; rest you
Let's see these pockets: the letters that he speaks of
May be my friends. He's dead; I am only sorry
He had no other death's-man. Let us see:
Leave, gentle wax; and, manners, blame us not:
To know our enemies' minds, we'ld rip their hearts;
Their papers, is more lawful.

Reads
'Let our reciprocal vows be remembered. You have
many opportunities to cut him off: if your will
want not, time and place will be fruitfully offered.
There is nothing done, if he return the conqueror:
then am I the prisoner, and his bed my goal; from
the loathed warmth whereof deliver me, and supply
the place for your labour.
'Your--wife, so I would say--
'Affectionate servant,
'GONERIL.'

O undistinguish'd space of woman's will!
A plot upon her virtuous husband's life;
And the exchange my brother! Here, in the

*purse: if you want to prosper, bury my body;
and give the letters which you will find on me
to Edmund Earl of Gloucester; look for him
amongst the British party: oh, too early death!*

*I know you well: a fair villain;
you were as helpful to your mistress' vices
as evil could want.*

What, is he dead?

*Sit down, father; rest.
Let's look in his pockets: the letters he speaks of
might help me. He's dead; I'm only sorry
he didn't have a different executioner. Let's see:
if you'll excuse me, gentle wax; and don't blame
our manners:
to know what our enemies think, we rip out their
hearts;
it's more lawful to rip open their letters.*

*"Let our two-way promises be remembered. You
have many
chances to kill him; if you're strong enough to
do it
you will find a good time and place. If he comes
back
victorious then nothing will happen; then I will
be a prisoner, with his
bed as my jail; rescue me from the despised
warmth of that, and give me an alternative with
you.
Your wife,
as I would like to say—
your affectionate lover,
Goneril."*

*Oh the limitless capacity of women for lust!
She plots against her virtuous husband's life,
planning to exchange him for my brother!*

141

sands,
Thee I'll rake up, the post unsanctified
Of murderous lechers: and in the mature time
With this ungracious paper strike the sight
Of the death practised duke: for him 'tis well
That of thy death and business I can tell.

GLOUCESTER
The king is mad: how stiff is my vile sense,
That I stand up, and have ingenious feeling
Of my huge sorrows! Better I were distract:
So should my thoughts be sever'd from my griefs,
And woes by wrong imaginations lose
The knowledge of themselves.

EDGAR
Give me your hand:

Drum afar off
Far off, methinks, I hear the beaten drum:
Come, father, I'll bestow you with a friend.

Exeunt

I'll bury you here in the sand, the unholy letters of murderous lechers; and when the time is right I will show this wicked letter to the Duke you've condemned. It's lucky for him that I can tell him about your plots.

The King is mad: how rigid my horrible senses are, that I'm still standing and can consciously feel my great sorrows! I'd rather be mad: that way my thoughts would be separated from my grief, and through self-deception I would not know about my sorrow.

Give me your hand:

I think I can hear a drum beating far off: come on, father, I'll leave you with a friend.

SCENE VII. A tent in the French camp. LEAR on a bed asleep,

Soft music playing; Gentleman, and others attending.

Enter CORDELIA, KENT, and Doctor

CORDELIA
O thou good Kent, how shall I live and work,
To match thy goodness? My life will be too short,
And every measure fail me.

Oh good Kent, how can my life and deeds match your goodness? My life will be too short, I could never live up to it.

KENT
To be acknowledged, madam, is o'erpaid.
All my reports go with the modest truth;
Nor more nor clipp'd, but so.

To be acknowledged by you, madam, is to be overpaid.
All my reports are nothing but the truth; not exaggerated or edited, just the truth.

CORDELIA
Be better suited:
These weeds are memories of those worser hours:
I prithee, put them off.

Let's get you some better clothes: these rags are reminders of those bad times: please, take them off.

KENT
Pardon me, dear madam;
Yet to be known shortens my made intent:
My boon I make it, that you know me not
Till time and I think meet.

Excuse me, dear madam; to reveal myself now would interfere with my plans: I ask you as a favour to not show that you know me until I think the time is right.

CORDELIA
Then be't so, my good lord.

Just as you wish, my good lord.

To the Doctor
How does the king?

How is the King?

Doctor
Madam, sleeps still.

Madam, he is still asleep.

CORDELIA
O you kind gods,
Cure this great breach in his abused nature!
The untuned and jarring senses, O, wind up
Of this child-changed father!

Oh you kind gods, repair the great wrongs that have been done to him!
Tune up the discordant and clashing mind of this father, changed by his children!

Doctor

143

So please your majesty
That we may wake the king: he hath slept long.

CORDELIA
Be govern'd by your knowledge, and proceed
I' the sway of your own will. Is he array'd?

Gentleman
Ay, madam; in the heaviness of his sleep
We put fresh garments on him.

Doctor
Be by, good madam, when we do awake him;
I doubt not of his temperance.

CORDELIA
Very well.

Doctor
Please you, draw near. Louder the music there!

CORDELIA
O my dear father! Restoration hang
Thy medicine on my lips; and let this kiss
Repair those violent harms that my two sisters
Have in thy reverence made!

KENT
Kind and dear princess!

CORDELIA
Had you not been their father, these white flakes
Had challenged pity of them. Was this a face
To be opposed against the warring winds?
To stand against the deep dread-bolted thunder?
In the most terrible and nimble stroke
Of quick, cross lightning? to watch--poor perdu!--
With this thin helm? Mine enemy's dog,
Though he had bit me, should have stood that night
Against my fire; and wast thou fain, poor father,
To hovel thee with swine, and rogues forlorn,
In short and musty straw? Alack, alack!
'Tis wonder that thy life and wits at once

*Would your Majesty agree
to our waking the King: he has been asleep a long time.*

*Follow your knowledge and go ahead
as you think is best. Is he dressed?*

*Yes, madam; as he slept so heavily
we put new clothes on him.*

*Be there, good madam, when we wake him up;
I'm sure he will be same.*

Very well.

Please come near. Play the music louder!

*Oh my dear father! Recovery, make
my lips your medicine; let this kiss
repair the violent damage that my two sisters
have done to your sacred person!*

Kind and dear Princess!

*Even if you hadn't been their father, your white
hair should have made them pity you. Was this a
face that should have been put out in the gales?
To stand up to the deep and terrible thunder?
To face the terrible quick stabs
of the furious lightning? To stand guard-poor sentry!-
with just this thin helmet? My enemy's dog,
even if it bit me, would have been allowed to stand
by my fire that night. And did you need, poor
father, to shack up with pigs and lost rogues
in thin and filthy straw? Alas, alas! It's amazing
that your life and your sanity didn't both end at*

144

Had not concluded all. He wakes; speak to him.

Doctor
Madam, do you; 'tis fittest.

CORDELIA
How does my royal lord? How fares your majesty?

KING LEAR
You do me wrong to take me out o' the grave:
Thou art a soul in bliss; but I am bound
Upon a wheel of fire, that mine own tears
Do scald like moulten lead.

CORDELIA
Sir, do you know me?

KING LEAR
You are a spirit, I know: when did you die?

CORDELIA
Still, still, far wide!

Doctor
He's scarce awake: let him alone awhile.

KING LEAR
Where have I been? Where am I? Fair daylight?
I am mightily abused. I should e'en die with pity,
To see another thus. I know not what to say.
I will not swear these are my hands: let's see;
I feel this pin prick. Would I were assured
Of my condition!

CORDELIA
O, look upon me, sir,
And hold your hands in benediction o'er me:
No, sir, you must not kneel.

KING LEAR
Pray, do not mock me:
I am a very foolish fond old man,
Fourscore and upward, not an hour more nor less;

once. He's waking up, speak to him.

You speak to him madam, that would be the most appropriate.

How is my royal lord? How is your Majesty?

You should not have pulled me out of the grave: you are a soul in heaven; but I am tied to a wheel of fire, so my own tears burn me like molten lead.

Sir, do you know who I am?

I know you are a ghost: when did you die?

He's still wandering!

He's barely awake: leave him alone for a while.

Where have I been? Where am I? Is this daylight? I have been very badly treated. I would die of pity if I saw this happen to someone else. I don't know what to say. I can't swear that these are my hands: let's see; I can feel this pinprick. If only I could be sure of my condition!

Oh, look at me, sir, and hold your hands over me in blessing: no, sir, you must not kneel.

Please, do not mock me: I am a very stupid senile old man, eighty and more, not an hour more or less; and, to speak plainly,

And, to deal plainly,
I fear I am not in my perfect mind.
Methinks I should know you, and know this man;
Yet I am doubtful for I am mainly ignorant
What place this is; and all the skill I have
Remembers not these garments; nor I know not
Where I did lodge last night. Do not laugh at me;
For, as I am a man, I think this lady
To be my child Cordelia.

CORDELIA
And so I am, I am.

KING LEAR
Be your tears wet? yes, 'faith. I pray, weep not:
If you have poison for me, I will drink it.
I know you do not love me; for your sisters
Have, as I do remember, done me wrong:
You have some cause, they have not.

CORDELIA
No cause, no cause.

KING LEAR
Am I in France?

KENT
In your own kingdom, sir.

KING LEAR
Do not abuse me.

Doctor
Be comforted, good madam: the great rage,
You see, is kill'd in him: and yet it is danger
To make him even o'er the time he has lost.
Desire him to go in; trouble him no more
Till further settling.

CORDELIA
Will't please your highness walk?

KING LEAR

*I fear I am not entirely sane.
I feel as if I should know you, and know this man;
But I am unsure because I am completely ignorant
of where I am; for the life of me I cannot remember these clothes; and I don't know where I stayed last night. Do not laugh at me; but
I would swear on my life that this lady is my child Cordelia.*

And I am, I am.

*Are your tears wet? Yes, indeed they are.
Please, don't cry:
if you have brought poison for me, I will drink it.
I know you do not love me; I remember now that your sisters have done me wrong, and they had no cause, which you have.*

There's no cause, no cause.

Am I in France?

You are in your own kingdom, sir.

Don't mock me.

*Be reassured, good madam: the great anger, as you can see, has died: but it is dangerous to try and go over the time he has lost.
Ask him to come inside; don't bother him further until he is more settled.*

Would your Highness come this way?

You must bear with me:
Pray you now, forget and forgive: I am old and foolish.

You must support me:
I pray that you can forget and forgive: I am old and foolish.

Exeunt all but KENT and Gentleman

Gentleman
Holds it true, sir, that the Duke of Cornwall was so slain?

Is it true, sir, that the Duke of Cornwall has been killed?

KENT
Most certain, sir.

Absolutely definite, sir.

Gentleman
Who is conductor of his people?

Who is leading his people now?

KENT
As 'tis said, the bastard son of Gloucester.

Rumour has it, the bastard son of Gloucester.

Gentleman
They say Edgar, his banished son, is with the Earl
of Kent in Germany.

They say Edgar, his exiled son, is with the Earl of Kent in Germany.

KENT
Report is changeable. 'Tis time to look about; the
powers of the kingdom approach apace.

There are different rumours. It's time to prepare;
the armies of the kingdom are coming on fast.

Gentleman
The arbitrement is like to be bloody. Fare you well, sir.

The outcome is likely to be bloody. Farewell, sir.

Exit

KENT
My point and period will be throughly wrought,
Or well or ill, as this day's battle's fought.

This could be full stop at the end of my life,
for better or for worse, depending how this battle goes.

Exit

147

Act 5

SCENE I. The British camp, near Dover.

Enter, with drum and colours, EDMUND, REGAN, Gentlemen, and Soldiers.

EDMUND (To a Gentleman, who goes out)
Know of the duke if his last purpose hold,
Or whether since he is advised by aught
To change the course: he's full of alteration
And self-reproving: bring his constant pleasure.

Find out from the Duke if his last order stands, or whether anything has happened since to make him change his mind: he's full of changes and self-reproach: bring back a firm order.

REGAN
Our sister's man is certainly miscarried.

Our sister's man has certainly come to harm.

EDMUND
'Tis to be doubted, madam.

I fear so, madam.

REGAN
Now, sweet lord,
You know the goodness I intend upon you:
Tell me--but truly--but then speak the truth,
Do you not love my sister?

Now, sweet lord, you know the good things I have planned for you: tell me—truthfully—even if I won't like it, do you or don't you love my sister?

EDMUND
In honour'd love.

I have an honourable love for her.

REGAN
But have you never found my brother's way
To the forfended place?

But you have never followed my brother into her bed?

EDMUND
That thought abuses you.

The thought is unworthy of you.

REGAN
I am doubtful that you have been conjunct
And bosom'd with her, as far as we call hers.

I fear that you have been joined with her and close to her bosom, in every sense of the phrase.

EDMUND
No, by mine honour, madam.

No, I swear it, madam.

REGAN
I never shall endure her: dear my lord,
Be not familiar with her.

I will not tolerate her: my dear lord, don't be friendly with her.

EDMUND
Fear me not:

Don't worry about me:

149

She and the duke her husband! | here she is and the Duke her husband!

Enter, with drum and colours, ALBANY, GONERIL, and Soldiers

GONERIL
[Aside] I had rather lose the battle than that sister
Should loosen him and me.

*I would rather lose the battle than have my sister
come between us.*

ALBANY
Our very loving sister, well be-met.
Sir, this I hear; the king is come to his daughter,
With others whom the rigor of our state
Forced to cry out. Where I could not be honest,
I never yet was valiant: for this business,
It toucheth us, as France invades our land,
Not bolds the king, with others, whom, I fear,
Most just and heavy causes make oppose.

*Our very loving sister, it is good to see you.
Sir, I have heard this; the King has come to his
daughter, with others who complained about the
harshness of our rule. I was never brave
when I could not be honest: this business
affects us as France is invading our land,
not out of arrogance but to support the King and
others whom
I'm afraid have very just and heavy grievances.*

EDMUND
Sir, you speak nobly.

Sir, you speak nobly.

REGAN
Why is this reason'd?

Why are you wasting your time arguing this out?

GONERIL
Combine together 'gainst the enemy;
For these domestic and particular broils
Are not the question here.

*Let's join together against the enemy;
these domestic and specific quarrels
are not the issue here.*

ALBANY
Let's then determine
With the ancient of war on our proceedings.

*Then let's confer
with our senior officers as to how to proceed.*

EDMUND
I shall attend you presently at your tent.

I will come to your tent shortly.

REGAN
Sister, you'll go with us?

Sister, you'll come with us?

GONERIL
No.

No.

REGAN
'Tis most convenient; pray you, go with us.

It would be for the best; please, come with us.

GONERIL
[Aside] O, ho, I know the riddle.--I will go.

Aha, I know what you're up to–I will come.

As they are going out, enter EDGAR disguised

EDGAR
If e'er your grace had speech with man so poor,
Hear me one word.

If your Grace ever speaks to such poor men, let me have a word.

ALBANY
I'll overtake you. Speak.

I'll catch up with you. Speak.

Exeunt all but ALBANY and EDGAR

EDGAR
Before you fight the battle, ope this letter.
If you have victory, let the trumpet sound
For him that brought it: wretched though I seem,
I can produce a champion that will prove
What is avouched there. If you miscarry,
Your business of the world hath so an end,
And machination ceases. Fortune love you.

Before you fight the battle, open this letter. If you win, then call the one who brought it with a fanfare: although I seem wretched, I can produce a champion who will confirm everything written there. If you fail, your time on earth would have come to an end, and all your plans will stop. Good luck to you.

ALBANY
Stay till I have read the letter.

Wait until I have read the letter.

EDGAR
I was forbid it.
When time shall serve, let but the herald cry,
And I'll appear again.

I was forbidden to do so. When the time is right, let the herald call, and I'll be back.

ALBANY
Why, fare thee well: I will o'erlook thy paper.

Why, good luck to you: I will read your paper.

Exit EDGAR

Re-enter EDMUND

EDMUND
The enemy's in view; draw up your powers.
Here is the guess of their true strength and forces
By diligent discovery; but your haste
Is now urged on you.

The enemy's in view; gather up your army. Here is the estimate of their true strength and forces through careful reconnoitring; but you must now make haste.

ALBANY

We will greet the time. | *I shall face the emergency.*

Exit

EDMUND
To both these sisters have I sworn my love;
Each jealous of the other, as the stung
Are of the adder. Which of them shall I take?
Both? one? or neither? Neither can be enjoy'd,
If both remain alive: to take the widow
Exasperates, makes mad her sister Goneril;
And hardly shall I carry out my side,
Her husband being alive. Now then we'll use
His countenance for the battle; which being done,
Let her who would be rid of him devise
His speedy taking off. As for the mercy
Which he intends to Lear and to Cordelia,
The battle done, and they within our power,
Shall never see his pardon; for my state
Stands on me to defend, not to debate.

I have sworn my love to both these sisters; each one is suspicious of the other, as the person who's been stung watches the adder. Which of them should I have? Both? One? Or neither? I won't be able to enjoy either of them if both of them remain alive: if I take the widow that will exasperate and make mad her sister Goneril; and I can hardly succeed with her, while her husband is alive. For now we'll use his authority for the battle; once that's over if she wants to get rid of him let her arrange for him to be quickly killed. As for the mercy which he intends to show to Lear and to ordelia, once the battle is over, and we have them in our power, they will never get his pardon; my position requires me to act, not to think.

Exit

SCENE II. A field between the two camps.

Alarum within. Enter, with drum and colours, KING LEAR, CORDELIA, and Soldiers, over the stage; and exeunt

Enter EDGAR and GLOUCESTER

EDGAR
Here, father, take the shadow of this tree
For your good host; pray that the right may thrive:
If ever I return to you again,
I'll bring you comfort.

Here, father, sit in the shadow of this tree for your shelter; pray that right will triumph: if I ever come back to again, I will look after you.

GLOUCESTER
Grace go with you, sir!

May God go with you, sir!

Exit EDGAR

Alarum and retreat within. Re-enter EDGAR

EDGAR
Away, old man; give me thy hand; away!
King Lear hath lost, he and his daughter ta'en:
Give me thy hand; come on.

Run, old man; give me your hand; run! King Lear has lost, he and his daughter are captured: give me your hand; come on.

GLOUCESTER
No farther, sir; a man may rot even here.

I will go no farther, sir; a man can stop here to rot.

EDGAR
What, in ill thoughts again? Men must endure
Their going hence, even as their coming hither;
Ripeness is all: come on.

What, having bad thoughts again? Men must suffer their going, just as they suffered their coming here; being ready for it is what's important: come on.

GLOUCESTER
And that's true too.

And that's true too.

Exeunt

153

SCENE III. The British camp near Dover.

Enter, in conquest, with drum and colours, EDMUND, KING LEAR and CORDELIA, prisoners; Captain, Soldiers, & c

EDMUND
Some officers take them away: good guard,
Until their greater pleasures first be known
That are to censure them.

*Let some of the officers take them away: guard them well,
until we know the wishes of the higher ones who will pass judgement on them.*

CORDELIA
We are not the first
Who, with best meaning, have incurr'd the worst.
For thee, oppressed king, am I cast down;
Myself could else out-frown false fortune's frown.
Shall we not see these daughters and these sisters?

*We're not the first people
to have meant the best and got the worst.
I am distraught for you, oppressed king;
otherwise, for myself, I could face down this ill fortune.
Will we not see these daughters and these sisters?*

KING LEAR
No, no, no, no! Come, let's away to prison:
We two alone will sing like birds i' the cage:
When thou dost ask me blessing, I'll kneel down,
And ask of thee forgiveness: so we'll live,
And pray, and sing, and tell old tales, and laugh
At gilded butterflies, and hear poor rogues
Talk of court news; and we'll talk with them too,
Who loses and who wins; who's in, who's out;
And take upon's the mystery of things,
As if we were God's spies: and we'll wear out,
In a wall'd prison, packs and sects of great ones,
That ebb and flow by the moon.

*No, no, no, no! Come on, let's go to prison:
we two on our own will sing like caged birds:
when you ask me for my blessings, I'll kneel down
and ask you for forgiveness: that's how we'll live, we'll pray, and sing, and tell old stories,
and laugh at vain fops, and hear poor scoundrels indulging in court gossip; we'll talk with them too, finding out who has lost and who has won; who's in, who's out; and we'll undertake to explain the mystery of things as if we were spies from God: and we'll outlive, in our walled prison, the cliques and parties of the great ones that rise and fall with the moon.*

EDMUND
Take them away.

Take them away.

KING LEAR
Upon such sacrifices, my Cordelia,
The gods themselves throw incense. Have I caught thee?
He that parts us shall bring a brand from heaven,
And fire us hence like foxes. Wipe thine eyes;
The good-years shall devour them, flesh and

*My Cordelia, the gods themselves will bless sacrifices like this. Do you understand?
We will never be parted except by someone bringing the fire of heaven
and smoking us out like foxes. Wipe your eyes; time will consume them, flesh and skin,*

154

fell,
Ere they shall make us weep: we'll see 'em starve
first. Come.

Exeunt KING LEAR and CORDELIA, guarded

EDMUND
Come hither, captain; hark.
Take thou this note;

Giving a paper
go follow them to prison:
One step I have advanced thee; if thou dost
As this instructs thee, thou dost make thy way
To noble fortunes: know thou this, that men
Are as the time is: to be tender-minded
Does not become a sword: thy great employment
Will not bear question; either say thou'lt do 't,
Or thrive by other means.

Captain
I'll do 't, my lord.

EDMUND
About it; and write happy when thou hast done.
Mark, I say, instantly; and carry it so
As I have set it down.

Captain
I cannot draw a cart, nor eat dried oats;
If it be man's work, I'll do 't.

Exit

Flourish. Enter ALBANY, GONERIL, REGAN, another Captain, and Soldiers

ALBANY
Sir, you have shown to-day your valiant strain,
And fortune led you well: you have the captives
That were the opposites of this day's strife:
We do require them of you, so to use them
As we shall find their merits and our safety
May equally determine.

before they weep again: until then, no tears. Come on.

*Come here, captain; listen.
Take this note;*

*Go and follow them to prison:
I have promoted you once; if you do
as this note orders, you will go on
to great things: you should know this, that men
have to act in a way that suits the times: to be softhearted
does not fit with the sword: this great task
is not open to debate; you say you'll do it,
or find some other way to get on.*

I'll do it, my lord.

Get going, and be happy when you have finished. Remember, I want it done at once; and make sure you do it just as I have instructed.

*I cannot pull a cart, or eat dried oats;
if it's work a man can do, I'll do it.*

*Sir, you have shown your bravery today,
and you had good fortune; you have our opponents in this day's battle as your prisoners;
I want them from you, so they can be treated
in such a way as their merits and our safety are suited.*

155

EDMUND
Sir, I thought it fit
To send the old and miserable king
To some retention and appointed guard;
Whose age has charms in it, whose title more,
To pluck the common bosom on his side,
An turn our impress'd lances in our eyes
Which do command them. With him I sent the queen;
My reason all the same; and they are ready
To-morrow, or at further space, to appear
Where you shall hold your session. At this time
We sweat and bleed: the friend hath lost his friend;
And the best quarrels, in the heat, are cursed
By those that feel their sharpness:
The question of Cordelia and her father
Requires a fitter place.

Sir, I thought it appropriate to send the old and miserable king into confinement with a guard watching over him; his age has an appeal to it, and his title even more so, which could turn the common people to his cause, and make our conscripts turn against us, their commanders. I sent the Queen with him; the same reason applied to her; now they are ready to appear before you tomorrow, or at a later time, wherever you hold your court. At the moment we are sweating and bloody; friends have lost friends, and the most justified causes, in the heat of battle, are cursed by those that suffer for them; the question of Cordelia and her father needs peaceful reflection.

ALBANY
Sir, by your patience,
I hold you but a subject of this war,
Not as a brother.

Sir, with all due respect, you are just a soldier in this war, not my equal.

REGAN
That's as we list to grace him.
Methinks our pleasure might have been demanded,
Ere you had spoke so far. He led our powers;
Bore the commission of my place and person;
The which immediacy may well stand up,
And call itself your brother.

That depends how we want to honour him. I thought that we should have shown him our favor before you said this. He led our armies, represented my title and my person; as he is my direct representative you might well call him your brother.

GONERIL
Not so hot:
In his own grace he doth exalt himself,
More than in your addition.

Not so fast: he has raised himself on his own merits more than through your titles.

REGAN
In my rights,
By me invested, he compeers the best.

As my representative, honoured by me, he equals the highest.

GONERIL
That were the most, if he should husband you.

That would be most true if he should marry you.

REGAN
Jesters do oft prove prophets.

Many a true line said in jest.

GONERIL
Holla, holla!
That eye that told you so look'd but a-squint.

*Hello, hello!
There's jealousy in your eye.*

REGAN
Lady, I am not well; else I should answer
From a full-flowing stomach. General,
Take thou my soldiers, prisoners, patrimony;
Dispose of them, of me; the walls are thine:
Witness the world, that I create thee here
My lord and master.

*Lady, I am not well; otherwise I would answer
you with angry words. General,
take my soldiers, my prisoners, my inheritance;
do what you want with them, with me; you have
won me: may everybody bear witness that I am
taking you as my lord and master.*

GONERIL
Mean you to enjoy him?

Do you mean to enjoy him?

ALBANY
The let-alone lies not in your good will.

You don't have the power to stop me.

EDMUND
Nor in thine, lord.

And neither do you, lord.

ALBANY
Half-blooded fellow, yes.

You bastard, I do.

REGAN
[To EDMUND] Let the drum strike, and prove
my title thine.

*Order the drum to be sounded, and claim my
title for yourself.*

ALBANY
Stay yet; hear reason. Edmund, I arrest thee
On capital treason; and, in thine attaint,
This gilded serpent.

*Wait a moment; listen to wisdom. Edmund, I
arrest you for the capital crime of treason; and,
along with you, this gilded serpent.*

Pointing to Goneril

For your claim, fair sister,
I bar it in the interest of my wife:
'Tis she is sub-contracted to this lord,
And I, her husband, contradict your bans.
If you will marry, make your loves to me,
My lady is bespoke.

*As to your claim, fair sister,
I block it in the interests of my wife;
she has given herself to this lord,
and I, her husband, forbid your marriage.
If you want to marry, you should offer yourself
to me, my lady is spoken for.*

GONERIL

An interlude!

This is like a play!

ALBANY
Thou art arm'd, Gloucester: let the trumpet sound:
If none appear to prove upon thy head
Thy heinous, manifest, and many treasons,
There is my pledge;

You are armed, Gloucester: sound the trumpet: if nobody appears to give evidence against you of your wicked, obvious and multiple treason then I promise you this;

Throwing down a glove

I'll prove it on thy heart,
Ere I taste bread, thou art in nothing less
Than I have here proclaim'd thee.

I'll prove in a fight, before my next meal, that you are absolutely what I have said you are.

REGAN
Sick, O, sick!

You are sick, sick!

GONERIL
[Aside] If not, I'll ne'er trust medicine.

If she's not, I'll never trust poison again.

EDMUND
There's my exchange:

Here's my reply:

Throwing down a glove

what in the world he is
That names me traitor, villain-like he lies:
Call by thy trumpet: he that dares approach,
On him, on you, who not? I will maintain
My truth and honour firmly.

If there's anyone in the world who calls me a traitor, he is a lying villain. call him with your trumpet: I will strongly fight for my truthfulness and honour, against anybody who dares to come, against him, against you, against anybody.

ALBANY
A herald, ho!

Herald, here!

EDMUND
A herald, ho, a herald!

A herald, here, a herald!

ALBANY
Trust to thy single virtue; for thy soldiers,
All levied in my name, have in my name
Took their discharge.

Put your faith in your own bravery; your soldiers were recruited in my name, and in my name they have been discharged.

REGAN
My sickness grows upon me.

I am feeling more sick.

ALBANY
She is not well; convey her to my tent.

She is not well; take her to my tent.

Exit Regan, led

Enter a Herald
Come hither, herald,--Let the trumpet sound,
And read out this.

Come here, herald – let the trumpet sound, and read this out.

Captain
Sound, trumpet!

Sound the trumpet!

A trumpet sounds

Herald
[Reads] 'If any man of quality or degree within
the lists of the army will maintain upon
Edmund,
supposed Earl of Gloucester, that he is a
manifold
traitor, let him appear by the third sound of the
trumpet: he is bold in his defence.'

'If any man of quality or rank within the army will give evidence that Edmund, supposed Earl of Gloucester, is a traitor many times over, let him present himself before the third trumpet call: he is adamant that he is innocent.'

EDMUND
Sound!

Blow!

First trumpet

Herald
Again!

Again!

Second trumpet

Herald
Again!

Again!

Third trumpet

Trumpet answers within

Enter EDGAR, at the third sound, armed, with a trumpet before him

ALBANY
Ask him his purposes, why he appears
Upon this call o' the trumpet.

Ask him what he means to do, why he appears in answer to the trumpet call.

Herald
What are you?
Your name, your quality? and why you answer
This present summons?

EDGAR
Know, my name is lost;
By treason's tooth bare-gnawn and canker-bit:
Yet am I noble as the adversary
I come to cope.

ALBANY
Which is that adversary?

EDGAR
What's he that speaks for Edmund Earl of Gloucester?

EDMUND
Himself: what say'st thou to him?

EDGAR
Draw thy sword,
That, if my speech offend a noble heart,
Thy arm may do thee justice: here is mine.
Behold, it is the privilege of mine honours,
My oath, and my profession: I protest,
Maugre thy strength, youth, place, and eminence,
Despite thy victor sword and fire-new fortune,
Thy valour and thy heart, thou art a traitor;
False to thy gods, thy brother, and thy father;
Conspirant 'gainst this high-illustrious prince;
And, from the extremest upward of thy head
To the descent and dust below thy foot,
A most toad-spotted traitor. Say thou 'No,'
This sword, this arm, and my best spirits, are bent
To prove upon thy heart, whereto I speak,
Thou liest.

EDMUND
In wisdom I should ask thy name;
But, since thy outside looks so fair and warlike,
And that thy tongue some say of breeding

Who are you?
What's your name, your rank? And why do you answer this summons?

You should know that my name is lost, ground down and poisoned by treason: yet I am as noble as the enemy I have come to take on.

Who is your enemy?

Who is representing Edmund Earl of Gloucester?

Himself: what do you have to say to him?

Draw your sword, so that if my speech offends your noble heart your arm can get revenge: here is mine. Look at it, it is the privilege of my position my oath and my knighthood to challenge you: I say, in spite of your strength, youth, possessions and position, despite your victorious sword and brand-new fortune, your heroism and your courage, you are a traitor; you are false to your gods, to your brother, and to your father; you are a conspirator against this illustrious Prince; and from the top of your head to the sole of your shoe you are stained with treachery. If you say you are not, this sword, this arm, and my greatest strength will be devoted to proving to your heart, which is what I'm speaking to, that you are a liar.

By rights I should ask your name; but since you look so fair and warlike in appearance, and the way you speak shows you have some breeding,

breathes,
What safe and nicely I might well delay
By rule of knighthood, I disdain and spurn:
Back do I toss these treasons to thy head;
With the hell-hated lie o'erwhelm thy heart;
Which, for they yet glance by and scarcely bruise,
This sword of mine shall give them instant way,
Where they shall rest for ever. Trumpets, speak!

although I would be within my rights to delay, through the rules of knighthood, I shan't do that: I throw these accusations at you; may your devilish lies swamp your heart; the lies have only glanced off me and hardly raised a bruise, I shall cut them a path into your heart with my sword, where they will stay forever. Sound the trumpets!

Alarums. They fight. EDMUND falls

ALBANY
Save him, save him!

Save him, save him!

GONERIL
This is practise, Gloucester:
By the law of arms thou wast not bound to answer
An unknown opposite; thou art not vanquish'd,
But cozen'd and beguiled.

This is treachery, Gloucester: by the laws of knighthood you are never obliged to accept a challenge from an unidentified opponent; you are not beaten, you have been misled and tricked.

ALBANY
Shut your mouth, dame,
Or with this paper shall I stop it: Hold, sir:
Thou worse than any name, read thine own evil:
No tearing, lady: I perceive you know it.

Shut your mouth, woman, or I'll gag you with this paper: wait, sir: you, too bad to be named, read about your own evil: don't go tearing it up, lady: I can see you know what is.

Gives the letter to EDMUND

GONERIL
Say, if I do, the laws are mine, not thine:
Who can arraign me for't?

So what if I do, I make the law, not you: who can charge me for it?

ALBANY
Most monstrous! oh!
Know'st thou this paper?

You monster! Oh! Do you know about this letter?

GONERIL
Ask me not what I know.

Don't ask me what I know.

Exit

ALBANY
Go after her: she's desperate; govern her.

Go after: she's desperate, control her.

EDMUND
What you have charged me with, that have I done;
And more, much more; the time will bring it out:
'Tis past, and so am I. But what art thou
That hast this fortune on me? If thou'rt noble,
I do forgive thee.

EDGAR
Let's exchange charity.
I am no less in blood than thou art, Edmund;
If more, the more thou hast wrong'd me.
My name is Edgar, and thy father's son.
The gods are just, and of our pleasant vices
Make instruments to plague us:
The dark and vicious place where thee he got
Cost him his eyes.

EDMUND
Thou hast spoken right, 'tis true;
The wheel is come full circle: I am here.

ALBANY
Methought thy very gait did prophesy
A royal nobleness: I must embrace thee:
Let sorrow split my heart, if ever I
Did hate thee or thy father!

EDGAR
Worthy prince, I know't.

ALBANY
Where have you hid yourself?
How have you known the miseries of your father?

EDGAR
By nursing them, my lord. List a brief tale;
And when 'tis told, O, that my heart would burst!
The bloody proclamation to escape,
That follow'd me so near,--O, our lives' sweetness!
That we the pain of death would hourly die

What you have accused me of, I admit to; that and much more; it will be revealed in time: it's gone, and so am I. But who are you who has triumphed over me? If you are noble I will forgive you.

If you forgive me I'll forgive you. I am just as highborn as you, Edmund; if more so, then you have wronged me even more. My name is Edgar, and I am your father's son. The gods are just, and they make tools to attack us out of our enjoyable vices: the dark and vicious act of conceiving you cost him his eyes.

You tell it how it is, it's true; the wheel has come full circle, and here I am.

I thought even the way you walked proclaimed a royal nobility: I must embrace you: may sorrow split my heart, if I ever hated you or your father!

Good prince, I know that's true.

Where have you been hiding? How did you find out about your father's misery?

By caring for him, my lord. Listen to a brief tale; and when I have told it I wish that my heart would burst! To escape the death sentence which was following me–oh, our lives are so sweet! We would rather feel the pain of death every

162

Rather than die at once!--taught me to shift
Into a madman's rags; to assume a semblance
That very dogs disdain'd: and in this habit
Met I my father with his bleeding rings,
Their precious stones new lost: became his guide,
Led him, begg'd for him, saved him from despair;
Never,--O fault!--reveal'd myself unto him,
Until some half-hour past, when I was arm'd:
Not sure, though hoping, of this good success,
I ask'd his blessing, and from first to last
Told him my pilgrimage: but his flaw'd heart,
Alack, too weak the conflict to support!
'Twixt two extremes of passion, joy and grief,
Burst smilingly.

EDMUND
This speech of yours hath moved me,
And shall perchance do good: but speak you on;
You look as you had something more to say.

ALBANY
If there be more, more woeful, hold it in;
For I am almost ready to dissolve,
Hearing of this.

EDGAR
This would have seem'd a period
To such as love not sorrow; but another,
To amplify too much, would make much more,
And top extremity.
Whilst I was big in clamour came there in a man,
Who, having seen me in my worst estate,
Shunn'd my abhorr'd society; but then, finding
Who 'twas that so endured, with his strong arms
He fastened on my neck, and bellow'd out
As he'ld burst heaven; threw him on my father;
Told the most piteous tale of Lear and him
That ever ear received: which in recounting
His grief grew puissant and the strings of life
Began to crack: twice then the trumpets sounded,
And there I left him tranced.

hour rather than die at once!—I changed myself into a madman's rags, taking on an appearance that even dogs hated: dressed like this I met my father with his bloody sockets, the eyes just recently torn from them; I became his guide, led him, begged for him, kept him from giving up; I never–what a mistake!–told him who I was, until half an hour ago, when I had armed myself; although I was hoping for this good result, I was not certain, so I asked him for his blessing, and told him about my journey from beginning to end: but his damaged heart was too weak to cope with the conflict between the two extremes of passion, joy and grief, and it burst with happiness.

This speech of yours has moved me, and some good may come of it: but go on, you look as if you have something else to say.

If there is more that is more sad, keep it to yourself; I am nearly ready to cry hearing of this.

This would have seemed to be the limit of sorrow; but something else far worse created more sorrow and exceeded it. While I was loudly mourning a man came in who, having seen me at my lowest ebb, rejected my hated society; but then, finding out who it was who suffered like this, threw his strong arms around my neck, and cried out as if he could burst the sky; he threw himself on my father, and told the saddest tale of him and Lear that anyone ever heard: as he was telling it his grief grew strong, and his heartstrings began to crack: then the trumpets sounded twice, and I left him there unconscious.

ALBANY
But who was this?

But who was this?

EDGAR
Kent, sir, the banish'd Kent; who in disguise
Follow'd his enemy king, and did him service
Improper for a slave.

Kent, sir, the exiled Kent; disguised he followed his hostile king, and served him in a way that would have been improper for a slave.

Enter a Gentleman, with a bloody knife

Gentleman
Help, help, O, help!

Help, help, O, help!

EDGAR
What kind of help?

What kind of help?

ALBANY
Speak, man.

Speak, man.

EDGAR
What means that bloody knife?

Will does that bloody knife signify?

Gentleman
'Tis hot, it smokes;
It came even from the heart of--O, she's dead!

It's hot, it smokes; it came from the heart of–oh, she's dead!

ALBANY
Who dead? speak, man.

Who is dead? Speak, man.

Gentleman
Your lady, sir, your lady: and her sister
By her is poisoned; she hath confess'd it.

Your lady, sir, your lady: and she has poisoned her sister; she has admitted to it.

EDMUND
I was contracted to them both: all three
Now marry in an instant.

I was engaged to them both: now all three are married at once.

EDGAR
Here comes Kent.

Here comes Kent.

ALBANY
Produce their bodies, be they alive or dead:
This judgment of the heavens, that makes us tremble,
Touches us not with pity.

Bring out their bodies, dead or alive; this judgement of the gods makes me tremble, but I have no pity for the victims.

Exit Gentleman

Enter KENT
O, is this he? | *Oh, is this him?*
The time will not allow the compliment | *There's no time for the pleasantries*
Which very manners urges. | *which manners demand.*

KENT
I am come | *I have come*
To bid my king and master aye good night: | *to say goodbye to my King and master;*
Is he not here? | *is he not here?*

ALBANY
Great thing of us forgot! | *What a great thing I have forgotten!*
Speak, Edmund, where's the king? and where's | *Tell us, Edmund, where's the King? And where's*
Cordelia? | *Cordelia?*
See'st thou this object, Kent? | *Do you see these things, Kent?*

The bodies of GONERIL and REGAN are brought in

KENT
Alack, why thus? | *Alas, what has happened?*

EDMUND
Yet Edmund was beloved: | *You see that somebody loved Edmund:*
The one the other poison'd for my sake, | *One poisoned the other for my sake,*
And after slew herself. | *and then killed herself.*

ALBANY
Even so. Cover their faces. | *That's how it was. Cover their faces.*

EDMUND
I pant for life: some good I mean to do, | *I am gasping for breath: I mean to do some*
Despite of mine own nature. Quickly send, | *good, in spite of my nature. Send someone*
Be brief in it, to the castle; for my writ | *quickly, hurry up about it, to the castle; for I*
Is on the life of Lear and on Cordelia: | *have ordered the death of Lear and Cordelia:*
Nay, send in time. | *send someone in time to stop it.*

ALBANY
Run, run, O, run! | *Run, run, oh, run!*

EDGAR
To who, my lord? Who hath the office? send | *Who are you telling, my lord? Who's got the*
Thy token of reprieve. | *job? Send*
| *something to show the reprieve is genuine.*

EDMUND

Well thought on: take my sword,
Give it the captain.

ALBANY
Haste thee, for thy life.

Exit EDGAR

EDMUND
He hath commission from thy wife and me
To hang Cordelia in the prison, and
To lay the blame upon her own despair,
That she fordid herself.

ALBANY
The gods defend her! Bear him hence awhile.

EDMUND is borne off

Re-enter KING LEAR, with CORDELIA dead in his arms; EDGAR, Captain, and others following

KING LEAR
Howl, howl, howl, howl! O, you are men of stones:
Had I your tongues and eyes, I'd use them so
That heaven's vault should crack. She's gone for ever!
I know when one is dead, and when one lives;
She's dead as earth. Lend me a looking-glass;
If that her breath will mist or stain the stone,
Why, then she lives.

KENT
Is this the promised end?

EDGAR
Or image of that horror?

ALBANY
Fall, and cease!

KING LEAR
This feather stirs; she lives! if it be so,

*Good thinking: take my sword,
give it to the captain.*

Hurry, as if your life depended on it.

*He has orders from your wife and me
to hang Cordelia in the prison, and
to blame her own despair,
saying she committed suicide.*

May the gods save her! Carry him away for a while.

*Howl, howl, howl, howl! Oh, you have hearts of stone:
if I had your tongues and eyes I would be wailing and crying
so that the skies would crack. She's gone forever! I know the difference between the living and the dead; she's as dead as earth. Lend me a mirror; if her breath mists or stains the crystal, well then, she is alive.*

Is this the last judgement?

Or a representation of that horror?

Let the skies fall and everything end!

This feather moves; she's alive! If it's the case,

It is a chance which does redeem all sorrows
That ever I have felt.

KENT
[Kneeling] O my good master!

KING LEAR
Prithee, away.

EDGAR
'Tis noble Kent, your friend.

KING LEAR
A plague upon you, murderers, traitors all!
I might have saved her; now she's gone for ever!
Cordelia, Cordelia! stay a little. Ha!
What is't thou say'st? Her voice was ever soft,
Gentle, and low, an excellent thing in woman.
I kill'd the slave that was a-hanging thee.

Captain
'Tis true, my lords, he did.

KING LEAR
Did I not, fellow?
I have seen the day, with my good biting falchion
I would have made them skip: I am old now,
And these same crosses spoil me. Who are you?
Mine eyes are not o' the best: I'll tell you straight.

KENT
If fortune brag of two she loved and hated,
One of them we behold.

KING LEAR
This is a dull sight. Are you not Kent?

KENT
The same,
Your servant Kent: Where is your servant Caius?

KING LEAR
He's a good fellow, I can tell you that;

that piece of luck would make up for all the sorrow that I have ever felt.

Oh my good master!

Please, go.

It is noble Kent, your friend.

A curse upon you, you're all murderers and traitors! I might have saved her; now she's gone forever! Cordelia, Cordelia! Stay awhile. Ha! What's that you say? She always spoke softly, gentle and quiet, an excellent thing in a woman. I killed the scum that was hanging you.

That's true, my lords, he did.

*I did, didn't I, my man?
I have seen the day when I could have made them dance
with my cutting light sword: I am old now, and that's taken my ability. Who are you? My sight is not very good: I should know you.*

*If fortune said that there were two people, one she loved and one she hated,
we see one of them here.*

This is a sad sight. Aren't you Kent?

*I'm him,
your servant Kent: where is your servant, Caius?*

He's a good fellow, I can tell you that;

167

He'll strike, and quickly too: he's dead and rotten.

KENT
No, my good lord; I am the very man,--

KING LEAR
I'll see that straight.

KENT
That, from your first of difference and decay,
Have follow'd your sad steps.

KING LEAR
You are welcome hither.

KENT
Nor no man else: all's cheerless, dark, and deadly.
Your eldest daughters have fordone them selves,
And desperately are dead.

KING LEAR
Ay, so I think.

ALBANY
He knows not what he says: and vain it is
That we present us to him.

EDGAR
Very bootless.

Enter a Captain

Captain
Edmund is dead, my lord.

ALBANY
That's but a trifle here.
You lords and noble friends, know our intent.
What comfort to this great decay may come
Shall be applied: for us we will resign,
During the life of this old majesty,
To him our absolute power:

he'll attack, and quickly too: he's dead and rotting.

No, my good lord; I am the very man—

I'll deal with that in a moment.

That has followed your sad steps ever since your fortunes began to change.

You are welcome here.

I am really the man: everything is unhappy, dark, and deadly.
Your eldest daughters have destroyed themselves, and are dead through despair.

Yes, that's what I think.

He doesn't know what he's saying: it's no use talking to him.

Very useless.

Edmund is dead, my lord.

That means hardly anything at the moment.
You lords and noble friends, listen to my wishes.
Anything that can bring comfort to poor Lear shall be given: as for me I will hand over, for as long as this old Majesty is alive, my absolute power to him:

To EDGAR and KENT
you, to your rights:
With boot, and such addition as your honours
Have more than merited. All friends shall taste
The wages of their virtue, and all foes
The cup of their deservings. O, see, see!

I shall give you two your rights: with all the additional rewards which your great deeds richly deserve. All friends shall be paid rewards for their virtue, and all enemies shall be punished as they deserve. Oh! Look, look!

KING LEAR
And my poor fool is hang'd! No, no, no life!
Why should a dog, a horse, a rat, have life,
And thou no breath at all? Thou'lt come no more,
Never, never, never, never, never!
Pray you, undo this button: thank you, sir.
Do you see this? Look on her, look, her lips,
Look there, look there!

And my poor fool is hanged! No, no, no life! Why should a dog, a horse, a rat, have life, and you have no breath? You'll never come back, never, never, never, never, never! Please, undo this button: thank you, sir. Can you see this? Look at her, look, her lips, look there, look there!

Dies

EDGAR
He faints! My lord, my lord!

He faints! My lord, my lord!

KENT
Break, heart; I prithee, break!

Break, heart; please, break!

EDGAR
Look up, my lord.

Look up, my lord.

KENT
Vex not his ghost: O, let him pass! he hates him much
That would upon the rack of this tough world
Stretch him out longer.

Do not torture his spirit: let him go! You would have to really hate him to stretch him out upon the rack of this harsh world any longer.

EDGAR
He is gone, indeed.

Yes, he's gone.

KENT
The wonder is, he hath endured so long:
He but usurp'd his life.

It's amazing he survived so long: he overthrew his life.

ALBANY
Bear them from hence. Our present business
Is general woe.

Carry them away. At the moment we have to deal with the general sorrow.

To KENT and EDGAR

Friends of my soul, you twain
Rule in this realm, and the gored state sustain.

KENT
I have a journey, sir, shortly to go;
My master calls me, I must not say no.

ALBANY
The weight of this sad time we must obey;
Speak what we feel, not what we ought to say.
The oldest hath borne most: we that are young
Shall never see so much, nor live so long.

Exeunt, with a dead march

*My dearest friends, you two
must rule this kingdom, and nurse the wounded
state back to health.*

*There is a journey, sir, I must shortly undertake:
my master calls me, I must not refuse.*

*We must do as this sad time dictates;
we must say what we feel, not what we ought to
say.
The oldest have suffered the most: we young
ones will never see as much, or live as long.*

Printed in Great Britain
by Amazon